# Bruise

A Novel

Adrian Markle

BRINDLE
AND GLASS

Copyright © 2024 by Adrian Markle
All rights reserved. No part of this publication may be reproduced, stored in a retrieval system, or transmitted in any form or by any means, electronic, mechanical, photocopying, recording, or otherwise, without the prior written permission of the publisher. For more information, contact the publisher at:
Brindle & Glass
An imprint of TouchWood Editions
touchwoodeditions.com

Edited by Kate Kennedy
Proofread by Senica Maltese
Interior design by Sara Loos
Cover design by David Drummond

CATALOGUING DATA AVAILABLE FROM LIBRARY AND ARCHIVES CANADA
ISBN 9781990071072 (softcover)
ISBN 9781990071102 (electronic)

TouchWood Editions acknowledges that the land on which we live and work is within the traditional territories of the Lkwungen (Esquimalt and Songhees), Malahat, Pacheedaht, Scia'new, T'Sou-ke and W̱SÁNEĆ (Pauquachin, Tsartlip, Tsawout, Tseycum) peoples.

We acknowledge the financial support of the Government of Canada through the Canada Book Fund and the Canada Council for the Arts, and of the Province of British Columbia through the British Columbia Arts Council and the Book Publishing Tax Credit.

This book is a work of fiction. Names, characters, places, and incidents are either products of the author's imagination or are used fictitiously. Any resemblance to actual events or locales or persons, living or dead, is entirely coincidental.

This book was printed using FSC®-certified, acid-free papers, processed chlorine free, and printed with soya-based inks.

Printed in Canada

28 27 26 25 24    1 2 3 4 5

For El, without whom neither this book nor I would be half what we are.

# Chapter 1

THE GREYHOUND BUS SHUDDERED IN place behind him, then died. The engine clinked as it cooled in the sea air. It would wait a while then go back, not to return for another two weeks. This was the end of the line and would probably soon be beyond it.

An empty chip bag tumbled across the parking lot.

Stone-grey clouds hung low overhead as if caught in the depression of the small town, much of which was built, wedge-shaped, in a gutter between two ridges. On one of the ridges, a hospital perched. And on the other side of that ridge, in shadow for the last half of the day, was the rest of the town. Stretching out in either direction were countless other little ridges and lonely beaches almost certainly littered with rotting, abandoned fishing gear.

Jamie already wanted to get back on the bus and go crawling back to whatever was left of his life in the city, if there was anything at all, but he didn't think he could even afford the ticket. It had cost him almost everything he had left just to get here.

So instead he let the streets carry him like trash in a river down toward the harbour. The road sloped sharply, the impact of his steps sending jolts of pain through his knee, and that was despite the surgery a few years ago. The houses were thin and tightly packed, white sides weathered grey and brown.

There were FOR SALE signs in front of a lot of them, but the signs had been up so long they were weather worn, some rotting. A number of the houses were fully boarded up, and many of the rest also seemed empty—no lights or sounds from within or smoke from the chimneys. In its heyday about two thousand people had lived here. Now it was obviously less. Far less, by the looks of it, and shrinking.

At the harbour, the sea surprised him with its vastness, its dark emptiness. It had been a long time since he'd really seen it. He'd forgotten the relentless sound of it. The slips where the fishermen kept their boats were mostly full, though it was almost noon. They'd all used to go out at sunrise and come back at sunset, so as a kid he'd only really seen them as specks shrinking against dawn or growing from the dusk. But now they just rocked in place while a bent old man walked without urgency between them, pulling sodden ropes to check the tightness of their knots.

It seemed the only thing they'd hauled out of the water here lately had been his father's body some months before, his flesh grey and yellow and wrapped in thin-blooded bruises, with lungs full of seawater and enough booze in his veins to kill a better man. Jamie hadn't actually been here to see him, but he wouldn't have bothered to look even if he had been. He'd heard some of the details in a voicemail and imagined the rest himself, and that was about all he needed to know.

There was almost no beach here, which was what had once made it so good for fishing. The ground fell away sharply from the shore, leaving a deep, natural harbour that the ships were safe to enter no matter how low in the water they rode with their haul, but it wasn't good for much else.

The wind was strong, common for April. Common for most months, actually. He pulled his coat tighter and looked up to the hospital—the building a relic from another time—then forced himself to lower his eyes. He wasn't ready for that yet, but he kept looking back to it. When he forced his gaze down for the half-dozenth time, he ducked into the only business he saw open, the bar called the Anchor, to remove it from his sight altogether.

What light came through the small, dirty windows was dead and grey. The bar was against one wall with stools in front of it, mostly full, and there were tables against the wall opposite, mostly empty. He stood in the doorway looking, until a woman shouted, "Close the door. Wind's up."

There were half a dozen men at the bar, each in a plaid shirt—varying colours and patterns, though most red and blue or red and black, and all sun-faded and fraying at the sleeves or collar—and high rubber boots, like they were going out to the boats, but the heaviness with which they sat on the stools belied the likelihood of that. They'd looked up at him as one when he'd opened the door, but not in the way he knew and missed. He sat in the empty stool closest to the door—the padding worn down to nothing—and set his bag down beside him. A mirror behind the bar had a collection of dusty Polaroids tacked around the frame and bottles on the shelves in front of it.

The bartender was the only woman there. She had a deep tan and brown hair, wavy and curly and wild. She was about his age, and strong. Lines of definition in her traps and pecs showed from the wide neckline of her shirt. He recognized her, probably from school, but that was the best he could do with that—it had been too long. And he probably hadn't done his memory any favours by taking all those hits to the head over the years, either. She was pretty, though. He opened his mouth to maybe say something about that to her, then stopped. It had been years since he'd had to speak to anyone he didn't already know, or at least who didn't already know him. He didn't know what to say to someone new, how to bridge that gap with strangers.

"What can I do for you?" She had a hard smile and a harder voice.

"Okay if I just sit a minute?" he asked.

"Sure. But this isn't the library; you can't just sit for free, or we'd be closed down just like they are."

"The library's closed?" He was strangely disappointed. He'd never gone, never had any desire too, but now that he knew he wasn't able to, he felt sad about it.

"Yeah, years now. What can I get you?"

He couldn't really fit his right hand in his jeans' pocket anymore, especially not sitting, so he patted the lump of change and notes and guessed at their value based on how much space it took up.

"Don't really drink. Can I get a glass of milk?"

There was an eruption of laughter from the old men in the bar. His right hand burned.

"You want *milk*?" she said.

He nodded. "Protein, calcium, vitamins B-Twelve and D."

"Don't get much call for milk, I'm afraid. I've got juice."

"All sugar. I guess a whisky then."

"Thought you couldn't drink?"

"Shouldn't. And probably won't. But . . ." But he had to get something to stay, and he'd be less tempted by that than the juice.

"What kind?" She gestured to the shelves behind her.

"Holy shit," he said. "Can I see that one? The Japanese one?"

"You either order the drink or you don't," she said, so flatly and firmly she'd obviously said it a thousand times before.

"Please."

She hesitated but passed the bottle to him. The label was thick, textured, rough under his thumb, with slick black strokes making Japanese characters. It was unopened. And a bit sticky.

"Why do you have this?"

"Old customer, Hiro, was exploring surfing spots around here for a few months."

"People surf here now?" Jamie asked.

"No, not here. Harbour's good for nothing but fishing boats, and not even them now. No, but places around here, maybe. Or at least he hoped to find some. He kept saying he wanted to discover the next new spot."

"All he discovered was that there ain't shit here now to discover," one of the men said.

"So he left."

"Could barely understand a fucking word from him," the same guy said. He was in his sixties. He'd have had to cut to make heavyweight—tall and strong and broad in the shoulders, but fat. Real fat. The kind of concentrated fat that comes with being old and undisciplined and those things compounding each other for years. His hair was grey and straggled out from under the base of his toque. He held his pint with his left hand; his right, which rested on the bar, was curled up, probably by arthritis—a knobby and uneven claw. Jamie winced when he saw it.

The bartender laughed. "Understood every third word sober," she said, "and every tenth drunk. Went on and on about this whisky, so I ordered it. But by the time it came in, he'd gone, and none of these cheap bastards will shell out for it."

"Now that was a funny Jap," the fat man said, eliciting a few laughs from the bar. The bartender shot the fat man a look and he pinched his lips shut, and Jamie opened his mouth to respond—it had been a long time since he'd tolerated language like that—but his voice stuck in his throat. He was used to feeling like he was in control in any environment he was in. Things happened because he allowed them. They didn't when he didn't. That didn't feel like the case anymore. He didn't know if it was because this place was different, or because he was. But he was not himself anymore, especially not here.

"I don't believe that's the appropriate term, Paul," said a little guy from down the end of the bar—much leaner and shorter, with a bit of a stammer. Maybe a hundred and fifty-five pounds. He was similarly weathered, but his eyes weren't dull.

Paul coughed. "CBC radio tell you that, Colin?"

Jamie ran his fingertips gently across the whisky label. "I worked in Japan, once. They gave me bottles of this."

"That what you want, then? Am I finally going to open it?"

The other men stared.

Jamie moved his hand again to the smallness of the lump of money in his pocket. He put the bottle back down in the bar. "What's cheapest?" he asked.

Paul exploded with laughter, the air in front of him filling with a mist of beer and spit. "They used to give me bottles of it!" he cried in a shitty impression of Jamie. His nose was swollen and red. He slapped the bar a few times, sending ripples through the beers.

Jamie felt the guffaws as a pulse in his temples. He wasn't used to being laughed at anymore. It reminded him of his father.

The bartender leaned toward him. "Worthy's is cheap." She poured him a measure. "On me."

The guys at the bar groaned indignantly.

"That was my father's drink," Jamie said. Coming in had been a mistake. He should have just been a man and gone straight up to the hospital.

As he stared at the whisky in the glass, he caught Paul smirking and shooting glances over to him, drawing in breaths then letting them go, clearly gearing up to say something hilarious.

Colin cut him off. "Easy there, Paul," he said. "The man

that you're preparing to antagonize is, I believe, a cage fighting middleweight champion of the world."

Paul got quiet and stared at Jamie, who knew what the old idiot was finally noticing. Tall, broad shoulders, big arms, a nose both flat and crooked, cauliflower ear, heavy caveman brow from scar tissue.

He felt the looks again, the more familiar kind.

The bartender seemed unsurprised. "What's a bigshot like you doing here, then?"

He held his hand out above the bar, extended his fingers approaching straight, brought them together in a fist as much as he was able. "Broke it in my last fight. I'd broke it before, but this time . . ." He trailed off. He'd talked about it a lot in the last several months with whoever's couch he'd been sleeping on, but they'd all been fighters; they'd had similar experiences and hadn't needed him to actually tell the story, so he hadn't. He wasn't sure he knew how, even. But the men's chatter did not return even though he stopped talking. He could hear the hum of the bar fridges.

"Every time I hit him," he started, surprised at himself, "there was pain shooting all the way up. Almost passed out. Imagine that—hitting someone in the face and *you're* the one that almost goes out. Fought most of the fight like that. Came up just short. But, next time." Even finished, he didn't know if he'd needed to say that, or if he'd just hated that silence.

"Guess that makes you the *ex*-champ then, huh?" Paul said.

"A middleweight champ," Jamie said. "Not *the* champ. There are lots of organizations, so lots of championships," he started. When he'd first been coming up, he'd had to explain who he was and what he did so many times it now happened almost automatically. "I fought for Kage Killers, the biggest organization in Canada, but my opponents come from all over the world, so it's a world championship, and it's mine. Still. And no one's ever going to take it from me. But this fight I'm talking about—think of it like winning the Calder cup in the AHL. And then fighting in Japan was me getting called up to the NHL, right into the playoffs. Twenty-five thousand people live. Major league money. And I got injured my first time out."

He hadn't had a drink in a long time. It was bad for training, but he supposed that wasn't an issue just now. He took a sip and it was hot on his tongue and stung the roof of his mouth. The glass felt loose and unsteady in his hand.

He'd actually been stripped of the belt since he'd been unable to defend it with his hand how it was. But he still *felt* like it belonged to him, since no one beat him for it, and he wasn't going to talk about that here, not with these people.

He was working up the will to head back out when her hand came down onto his arm.

"So tell us the story then," she said.

The other men turned toward him, even Paul.

"He's an Olympian, Tamura," Jamie said, as quickly, almost urgently, as before. "Judo. Handsome guy, too. Honor Fighting Championships wanted to make him a superstar, and they brought me in to be his debut opponent. I'm foreign, a champ in another organization, and I've been uglied up some, so I look legit. Be a hell of a coming-out party if he could beat me."

"*If?*" Paul said, chucking again.

"Well, they brought him along too fast. He wasn't ready, and I had him dead to rights, until . . ." He held up his hand again. It was swollen and discoloured—a few thin lines of that dark angry blood rose to the surface near joints, but it was mostly a gentler colour, in places either piss-yellow or lilac—starting at the base of his thumb and stretching out across the back of his hand to the base of his pinkie.

"He's been getting a lot of shine since. He's a contender already, and making money. But, good; the more he gets now, the more I can take from him when we run it back."

"None of that explains what you're doing *here*, though," the bartender said.

He was only half listening, his head still in Japan. After a moment he returned his hands to his lap and said, "I grew up here."

"Really," Paul said. "Who's your old man?"

He'd been wondering if people here would've known him, if this would've turned out to be the only place in the world besides the gym where anyone knew who he was. But he'd been gone from here a long time, and he was different now. And the people who'd definitely have remembered him, his brother and father... well, he wasn't surprised they hadn't talked about him much, after what had happened.

He shook his head. "It was a while ago. Doubt you'd know him."

"Place this size? Try me," Paul said.

Colin drank his beer, eyes roaming the ceiling. The bartender looked to the floor. They knew. They didn't want to say it.

"Chuck Stuart," he said.

The men at the bar leaned slightly away.

"Jesus," Paul said, absently running his fat fingers across the scar under his eye. He cast a quick glance back over his shoulder.

"Oh, you're that boy that ran away," one of the other men said.

The bartender put her hand on his arm again. "You come back for the funeral?"

"If you did, you missed it," Paul said. "By quite a while. Don't think you were alone in missing it, though."

"Not here for him," he said. "Just here. Thanks for the drink," he added. He stood, his whisky untouched but the one sip.

He looked at the collection of faded and liquor-stained Polaroids pinned to the mirror frame. They were of people who'd been barred, usually blurry and from a bit of a distance. They were indignant fisherman mostly, some shitty kids, some furious women. But in one photo, blocked at first by the bottle that had been taken down for him, a man posed with a wide, defiant smile. A line of blood ran down from his nose, spread across his teeth, and poured over his bottom lip and down his chin—almost the shape of a cross.

It was his brother, head shaved and face narrow and axe-like. Pinned beneath the photo was a small piece of paper that said SID STUART – VIOLENCE, with a small drop of what looked like blood after the letters like a period.

RIGHT HAND RESTING IN HIS coat pocket like a sling, he walked up the hill to the hospital. He swore at himself for having gone on and on about his comeback and Tamura, when obviously nobody gave a shit and they'd just been humouring him.

The hospital was in an old repurposed French colonial house that the regional health department had been given in a trust by the last living heir of one of the first big trading families out this way who, when riddled with cancer, traded her home for the privilege of not having to die in the city. People called it a hospital because once it was one, but for a long time now it had been more of a small clinic with a few long-term care beds in the otherwise-empty second floor. Paint flaked from every section that wasn't exposed brick, and brick dust drifted from every section that was. It was huge and had three floors above ground, but most of the windows on the top two floors were boarded up now. The reception desk was currently unstaffed, so he walked past it and down the second hall to the third office on the right—a route he'd once walked almost daily. The door was ajar. At the desk was a man about Jamie's age. He wore a nice blue button-down and had a belly on him. His feet were on the desk, and he was pawing a fork at the bottom of a Styrofoam cup of noodles.

"Feet," Jamie said, and he inclined his head to the ground. The man slowly and hesitantly took his feet off the desk.

"Can I help you?" the man asked, tense.

"This is Doctor Carroll's office."

The man relaxed and smiled. "Ah, yes. Still get that occasionally." He laughed a bit nervously. "Ha. End of the hall on the left."

"Sorry," Jamie said, his face flushing.

The door at the end of the hall had her name on it. He knocked. There was a rustling behind the door, and he fought a sudden and unexpected urge to run. He almost hoped that she hadn't heard him. Then the door opened.

Her face, thinner than he remembered, rippled with surprise. She still wore an immaculate white coat over a suit, still tied her hair, now white, straight back. She opened her arms as if to hug him, but instead extended her hand for him to shake at the last second. He kept his right hand tucked in his pocket and gave her his left. She turned her hand upside down and took his that way, and it was still the least awkward handshake he'd had in years.

"Come," she said, and led him back to reception. "Look." She gestured to the desk, behind which a woman was now working.

"I'm sorry," he said. "You must be so busy. I totally understand. I didn't mean to barge in. I just thought... That's fine."

She looked at him with that mix of affection and pity. "No, James, *look*." She was the only one who'd ever called him James, except his mom, and he wasn't sure he even remembered that right. There was a plaque on the wall behind the reception desk—a brass medallion engraved with a pair of boxing gloves and his name on dark wood.

He leaned forward and squinted at it before looking down at his filthy shoes. "Those, uh, aren't the kind of gloves I wear."

"Oh, I know, James. But I could not find anyone who could engrave those little things you wore. In any case, you did not respond to my invitation for a ceremony, which I considered your opportunity to consult on the design. I didn't use any of the money you sent for this, by the by. I paid myself."

He looked back at the plaque. It was small, but the light wrapped around the brass in a way that made it catch the eye.

"Do you have time to sit?" she asked. "I was just making tea."

She assured him she'd be back in a second, and he stood stiffly just inside her office door. Despite her office having been moved, it was still set up largely how he remembered. There was a large window, due to the building having once been a house, but the bottom half was painted over with white and it was hung with thick curtains. There was an examination table, cupboards and a sink, a small blue plastic chair in the corner, a table with pamphlets, and her desk, in front of which were two office chairs.

She returned with a tea for herself and coffee for him, took a seat behind her desk, and gestured for him to sit.

He dropped his bag and sat in the little blue chair against the wall and felt like he was fourteen again. He slouched. He hadn't slouched in years.

"So," she said, "let me see it."

"See what?"

"The hand that's keeping you from fighting. The one you wouldn't take out of your pocket."

"You know, Olympians don't shake hands at all. And it's fine, really. It's getting there. I'm just trying to be safe. Vigilant."

"They do that to avoid catching a cold, James. Or the flu." She rolled her chair over to him and flattened her palm, expectantly, like she had once half-a-life ago, after Dex, when Jamie'd got in a fight at school and his hand swelled up like a balloon and she'd poked it and scolded him and made him tea. When he'd left that day, he'd called her Mom by accident. She'd been kind enough not to acknowledge it, but he'd still run out and hadn't come back for weeks.

He eased out his fist and rested it on her palm. Her hands were cold, the skin loose. But they were sure and confident like he had only ever been in the ring. She explored his hand, pressed and poked and pulled, wordlessly gauging his reactions as she did.

"What do you understand your situation to be?" she asked, slipping into that neutral, even tone. "And what do you understand your possibilities to be?"

He sat up. He knew this. "Always going to be easier to break next time than last time, so I have to be increasingly careful." He rattled it off like he'd been asked to memorize it for school. His doctor in the city, Webb, worked with a lot of athletes, and Jamie knew that Webb sometimes overstated things because of how bad everyone always wanted to get back in the gym, so he made things sound worse than they were, so they'd behave. "And the doc said that I've got to take it easy for a while, obviously. So that's why I'm here. Just resting. Just for a bit. Look in on... And then I'll head back to the city. And then we'll see."

"We have seen. I'm seeing now. I don't even need to X-ray, though we should schedule one. You have broken multiple bones, multiple joints. Multiple times. Your hand is one big fracture. Because it seems you have never let it heal properly, it *cannot* heal properly. If you continue making it worse, it will reach a point where—"

He jerked it back into his pocket. Each time his hand had broken, it had broken worse. Recovery took longer and longer. A few weeks at first. Then months. About a year the last time. There were twenty-seven bones in the hand, and he'd broken more than half of them at some point, and most of those more than once. But it had always healed.

"I just... came to say hi," he mumbled.

"James, it will reach a point where you will not be able to use it at all, for anything. We'll need tests, but I can tell already that you have chronic fractures and chronic inflammation." She went back around the desk to her chair. "Surgery will likely allow you to regain day-to-day function, but you... you know you won't fight again, yes? I'm sorry, James. Your hand will break on the first hard punch. And with one, two more breaks, even surgery may not allow you to regain that day-to-day function we're considering now."

He'd had similar conversations with Webb, but Jamie'd figured that gropey old quack was just telling him what he needed to be told so he'd live right for a while. He'd brushed it off. But Doctor Carroll had never lied to him, not even when he was a kid and he'd wanted her to. Others had said similar things before but when *she* said it, he had to listen. He had to.

It felt like the room was closing in on him, and there was a sharp, drawn-out ringing growing in his ears, pushing every other sound out. That had happened to him a few times in the last year or two, but he'd never been happy for it until now. She dabbed at her eyes. She was still talking to him. Why was she sad? She was sorry? But she wasn't the one who . . .

"No," he said, his voice and resolution wavering. "No, I just have to . . ." but he didn't remember anymore what he could do to make it better, was no longer sure if he believed there was anything at all.

She kept saying "I'm sorry" over and over. He still couldn't hear, but he recognized the shape of those words. He sat, blinking and looking out the window and flexing his fist as much as he was able. He stood up. He shook his head. The noise in his ears was the sound of a bell calling endlessly for the end of a round, one moment of conclusion ringing out and out forever.

## Age Thirteen

Single file, they stepped gingerly across the chunks of rough, grey rock that acted as a bridge between the beach and the field they'd just been marched through. The rocks were wet, and the wind was up. There was no one else on the beach. The sky, waves, sand, and stone were all colourless in the November air. Jamie looked past his older brother, Sid, at their father, who led them. He watched every unsure step the old man took and wished one of his half-drunk stumbles would end in a fall. His younger brother, Dex, followed behind him.

On the beach, the boys stripped down to their jeans and kicked their shoes off. The salt wind lashed at them and the boys turned their bare backs on the sea, at least keeping it from their eyes.

Their father placed himself between the boys and the dull-coloured long-grass field that writhed in the wind. He pulled his shirt and coat over his head in one motion and threw them down on the cold, clay-thick sand, where they landed with a dull thud. He tilted his head, confused. Then, almost giddy, picked the damp mass of clothes back up and fished his hand into it until he came out with an old flask. He let the clothes fall again. The flask was sterling silver. Inherited. Dull all over but for the ridge on the cap and the spot on its breast where his thumb had worn it into a polish. He drank about half of it in one, then closed and dropped that too.

Their father pulled his jeans as far up his calves as they'd go, then dragged his bare foot through the sand, cutting a jagged circle around himself, as Jamie imagined his father had done before him and his father before him.

He and his brothers flamingoed their legs, leaving sandy footprints on the inseams of their jeans.

"Well," their father said. "Okay, then."

It was Sid who stepped forward first. It always was. He rubbed his hand across his shaved head, shorter on one side than the other; Jamie had been running the clippers over Sid's head that morning when the old man had crashed out of his room and told them they were going down to the beach, now.

Sid clenched his jaw, rushed into the circle, and threw himself at the old man. He was fifteen, the only one that even approached their father's height.

Jamie held his breath. They were all three down there, all three stuck and having to fight, but only Sid had much of a chance. If he won, they could get out of this weather, go home. If he didn't, Jamie and Dex would take turns losing until he was ready to try again.

Sid slammed into their father, the larger man barely moving. They scrambled a bit, heads eventually resting on each other's right shoulders, as if they danced or wept. They each snaked their arms inside the other's, over and over, trying to get to the position where both arms were under their opponent's armpits at once, for leverage. Sid got there first, getting the old man almost in a bear-hug, and then he arched and twisted his back as much as he could, trying to take his father's weight and pivot it on his hip, to take his strength away from him.

All he had to do was throw him outside the circle, just once, for this all to be over.

Their father's feet slowly lifted from the ground.

Dex grabbed Jamie's hand, squeezed it in anticipation, his grip icy.

Jamie held his breath. The wind stopped roaring. The sea stopped crashing. The only sound was the crack-voiced grunt that escaped his brother as he struggled. Sid was two years older and two years bigger and two years stronger than Jamie, but the muscles in his narrow back shook under the strain of trying to carry the old man's weight. Sid held their father mostly aloft—his toes dragged across the sand—and stumbled two steps back toward the edge of the circle before his strength waned.

The ball of their father's foot crashed back down into the sand and all the sound of the world came rushing back to them. He spun and planted his other foot and sent Sid tumbling out of the circle just like that, barrelling across the sand toward the waves.

Jamie leapt at the old man before he'd had a chance to stop his coarse laugh. Jamie wasn't usually strong enough to win if his father wasn't too tired or drunk, but sometimes he could catch him by surprise. The old man turned and met him in the air and threw him sprawling out over the beach. The sand was hard and rough and left him with scrapes across his shoulder where he landed. Jamie picked himself and sucked the damp air into his lungs. He was wet now, too, and what little heat he'd had left in him disappeared quickly into the wind. He imagined himself in the future, hardened from this all, able to stand up against their dad or anyone like him, the way Sid tried to do for him and Dex.

Dex took a few small steps forward, his shaggy hair whipping wildly. He was the nicest of them, but the most feral looking—crooked teeth and wild hair. He walked forward and pressed himself into their father's leg, wrapped his arms around his thigh, and pressed his head against his hip. He just stood there, not even really trying to wrestle, just happy for the warmth. Happy for the hug. But he was good at it, too, at "tying up," even if that was rarely his real intention. Dex had a way of holding on with everything he had, not saving anything for later. It was a hell of time trying to get him off when he'd decided to hold on. Their father slid his hand down in between his leg and the boy's chest and, after straining a second, peeled him off with a backhand that sent him rolling away. Dex picked himself up and brushed wet sand from his pale skin. He should have known better—you left the sand on; it formed a shell, helped keep you warm on a long day.

A lone blue and white fishing boat chugged past. There was no one on deck. A dog barked from somewhere on the other side of the hill, and a snatch of a sound that could have been a person shouting answered back to it. Seabirds called out to the sky from the rocks on the west side of the beach.

Sid still lay on his back, heaving for breath. He must have got the wind knocked out of him. He pressed his hands up into his abdomen, almost as if reaching to manually restart his lungs. He would not be getting up to take his turn.

Their father used the pause in the action to pull another drink from the flask, and Jamie looked past him at the jagged rocks that connected the beach to the long brown grass, on the other side of which, eventually, was home. How far would he get if he just ran?

"She's not coming," their dad spat. "Look all you want. I've looked. She ain't. So look *here*, boy. Look at me here in front of you, not over there for some skirt to hide behind."

He was right. She wasn't coming. Not ever.

Jamie rushed forward and drove his shoulder into his father's stomach, and the old man's grunted breath washed over him, whisky sour, and Jamie was tumbling back over the beach. He didn't get up, just looked again to the long grass that waved in the wind like skirts.

**THE SUN WAS RARELY MORE** than a dim pulse behind the thick bank of clouds that blanketed the sky, but it was clearly dropping toward the horizon. Their father sat in the shallow pit their feet had pounded into the sand, laughing to himself occasionally and waiting for one of his boys to try him again. The flask was empty.

Dex sat nearby, legs crossed, their dad's coat wrapped around his shoulders, little white fingers sticking out at the neck. He wouldn't have gotten away with that when they'd first come down, but as the afternoon pressed on their father almost forgot he was there, his attention sticking with his older boys when it was on any of them at all.

Jamie spit blood into the sand. He'd bitten his tongue. "Th-this is s-s-stupid," he said, teeth chattering. It had been a while since he'd stepped into the divot they'd made, since he'd felt the heat of conflict, but he was feeling drawn to it. When the days drew on, the struggle became the most comfortable thing about being down there. "I want to go home," he said.

"Any time you like," his father said, and laughed. "All you've got to do is win once. You think *I'm* hard on *you*, but when my dad used to take me to the beach to wrestle . . ." he said, trailing off. "Well, it never even used to make me late for lunch. Jesus, you boys'd have to sleep out here sometimes if I didn't take pity on you."

"Maybe you're just a shit teacher," Sid said. He never stood for insults, even when he really should have. He climbed back to his feet and walked to the edge of the divot. Scraped raw by the sand, his skin was a canvas of pink and red swipes.

"You little shit," their father said. He struggled to stand, but Sid was on him, swinging. He did his best to hold his father down with his left arm and cracked his thin right arm through the air like a whip into the old man's face, over and over. Finally, their father gained his footing and straightened up and drove his fist square into Sid's nose. It erupted with blood, and Sid rocked back on his heels and tipped like a falling tree flat onto the sand. He covered his face with his hands, but otherwise didn't move except to suck in air.

Their father stood, heaving, then stomped over to Sid and stood over him, breathing, fists curled. "I'm trying to help you!" he shouted. "Don't you see?" He cocked his fist back and held it, shook his head, and let it go. He marched over to where Dex sat amongst the discarded clothes. Dex scrambled out of the way just as their father's foot swung through the pile, sending the clothes, his, theirs, out toward the sea.

"I'm trying to fucking help you," he muttered. He walked off toward the rocks, which Jamie hoped he'd fall from but knew he wouldn't.

Jamie ran out into the surf. It was freezing, but he'd felt numb for some time. He fished out what clothes he could before they drifted too far from his reach.

## Chapter 2

FOR PRETTY MUCH HIS ENTIRE adult life, if he got bad news he'd have gone to the gym, if he wasn't there already. It was the same if he got good news. The gym was where things made sense. But the gym seemed another country from here, and besides, he wasn't really welcome there anymore. The bar seemed to do that same job for those old guys he'd seen earlier, but that wasn't his space. He hadn't seen how to connect to that. In fact, it had only made him feel worse, which left him only one other place to go.

He'd gotten lost on the way from the hospital, marching down street after street waiting for one to feel familiar. He'd almost accidentally left town before finding his way. The house was the standard narrow build, the white exterior stained brown and grey, with just enough space out front for a couple bikes, though they'd never actually had bikes. In the back there was a little yard with a shed. That was it. There was nothing but room in this part of the country, though none of it made it to the houses. Maybe whoever first built them had expected the town to grow more than it had, so were extra tight-fisted about space. Maybe they didn't think they'd have the time to maintain it. Or maybe they just didn't think the people who'd live here deserved much.

Except that the house looked smaller than he remembered, his brother seemed to have kept it exactly the same. If his brother was even here anymore. He realized only then that he had no idea what had happened to the house, legally speaking, after their father had died. No one had been in touch with him, and he hadn't thought to reach out—not that he'd have known who to contact if he'd wanted to.

He listened for any sound from inside, went up onto his tiptoes to see through the little arched window at the top of the door, but he wasn't tall enough without jumping, and his knee was already too sore to do that from all the walking on uneven ground he'd done that morning. The handle turned. He wanted to shoot back from the door, create some distance, but his legs froze in a way they never had in a fight, and he just watched the thing swing inward.

Sid was taller. An inch or two taller than Jamie. Of course he'd have grown, *of course*, but it was something else to see. He was still thin though. Not the thinness of growing faster than you can eat, but an unhealthy, end-of-a-weight-cut thin. His cheekbones were sharp, his eyes were sunken, and one wore the late sunset of an old bruise. He wore track pants and a baggy T-shirt. His bony arms were crowded with blurry tattoos. His dark hair was short—not business short, just a while between shavings—and receding some. It lay flat, came naturally to a point down the middle of his forehead. He had a beard, reddish, which added a bit of square-jawed shape to his face.

Jamie didn't know why, but he tensed for his brother to charge at him. But Sid didn't. And he wanted to reach out and wrap his brother in an embrace like how he used to do with Mo and Robbie like it was nothing—like how he must have done with Sid once, in their childhood. But he didn't, and he didn't know why.

A lot of time passed between them. His brother was stone faced. As a kid, Sid had worn everything on the outside and had no ability or desire to hide anything of himself. But sometime between then and now he'd acquired both.

"You okay?" Jamie asked, finally.

"What?" His brother squinted at him.

"Just wondering if you were...okay."

"Why wouldn't I be okay?"

Jamie looked back out to the empty street.

Sid turned and walked back into the house. He left the door open. He was barefoot. "Coffee?" he said. He walked down the narrow hall past the living room into the laminate kitchen. He didn't react to the cold under his feet. At least they still had that in common.

His brother shrunk into the house, passing in and out of his view as he moved around the kitchen. The kettle began to growl.

"Don't leave the door open like that. What, were you raised in a barn?" he asked, then laughed. "Well . . ." He laughed some more. His laugh was thin too.

Jamie stepped in and dropped his bag against the wall. The carpet had faded. The house smelled like cigarette smoke.

He pulled his shoes off by stepping on the heel and lifting his foot out. Tying and untying every day was too much hassle now, with his hand. The shoes were stretched and sagging. The soles let in the water, so they smelled musty. He'd been given them—and a lot of other clothes—as a part of a sponsorship deal with a big sports equipment store in the city, but that deal had expired a while ago and he didn't have money for new ones.

He suddenly couldn't remember if he'd ever bought his own clothes. As a kid, his mom—and, he supposed, even his dad at some point—had done that for him, and when he'd run away he'd stolen from washing lines or been given things by charities, and as soon as he'd settled into the gym, Mo had taken care of that kind of thing.

The laminate was worn down in front of the fridge, the sink, the kettle. It was a map of where the Stuarts had stood. Jamie stayed at the edge of the room.

"Sorry," Jamie said.

"For what?"

"For just showing up, I guess. Out of the blue."

Sid shook his head. "That's not a thing to apologize for," he said. He opened the kitchen window and dumped a full ashtray out, some ash blowing back in and spreading over the sink and counter.

"You smoke," Jamie said.

"I quit once, but here we are."

"Remember when he caught us smoking?"

"Threatened to set me on fire with his favourite lighter, he ever saw it again."

"Made me smoke a whole pack until I threw up," Jamie said. "And then he laughed at me." He forced a short laugh. "He was such a bastard."

"Worked, didn't it?"

"Obviously not on you."

Sid shrugged. "Guess I must have wanted to burn."

The kettle reached a boil, and Sid took two mugs from the cupboard and mixed Jamie a cup of instant coffee. He held up the jar it came in, black with gold writing. "The good stuff," he said. He smiled. Then he hissed, "Shit. I put milk in. I didn't even ask. Is that okay? Or are you one of those soy people now?"

"Milk's fine."

Sid nodded again and exhaled, relaxed a bit. "Sugar?" He gestured to an almost torso-sized bag on the counter. The top was roughly torn open, the seam of the tear dragging downward at one corner like skin peeled away from the edge of a fingernail.

He shook his head. "Don't really eat sugar."

Sid scooped himself several heaps with a spoon already in the bag and dropped it back in, still wet with coffee. "So," he said.

Jamie also took a drink. The coffee was cheap, sour. He nodded. "S'good."

Sid smiled, the corners of his mouth curling up devilishly. The cupboard door still hung open. The drinking glasses were mostly pints, most with faded branding on them from this beer or that, most likely stolen from bars.

They sat quiet in the living room not really making eye contact. Jamie pressed the mug down into his upturned right hand on his lap, as if to flatten it back into shape. The heat helped relieve the ache, even as the pressure created it. Jamie sat in the chair, sun-bleached and floral, and Sid on the sofa, black faded grey.

Sid drew deep, conspicuous breaths. Jamie cast his eyes over furniture, the mantle above the bricked-up fireplace and the small unframed photos it bore, the bookshelf, the books, and tried to remember what of it had been in the room last time he had been. Most of it. Maybe all.

He heard his brother's sharp inhales. He heard water dripping from the faucet in the kitchen, droplets exploding on the steel bottom of the sink. He heard the hedges in the back garden rustle. And he heard his brother's defeated exhales. The house creaked. The silence grew to occupy so much space in the room that Jamie felt like it was getting crowded.

"Right," Jamie said, disturbing the silence, and he winced at the sound of it, reeling as if it were a blow he'd not seen coming. He moved to stand despite not having anywhere to go, but Sid was up like a shot.

"No," Sid said. He'd already closed the distance, pushed Jamie back down into the chair, and collected the mug. Sid was stronger than he looked, but Jamie still had to allow himself to be moved. Sid hurried out of the room, calling,

"I know what to do." Jamie heard the mugs crashing into the sink, cupboards opening and closing, and the slap of Sid's bare feet on the laminate.

He returned with a bottle of whisky in one hand and two mugs in the other, pinched together between finger and thumb. He set the mugs and bottle on the coffee table, then dragged the table and one end of the sofa a bit closer to Jamie. He dropped back down onto it, held up the bottle. It was Worthy's. A big bottle. A full litre.

He hadn't seen Worthy's in years, and now twice in a day.

"Remember?" Sid said. He smiled.

He and Sid must have remembered things very differently.

"How could I forget?"

Sid leaned forward and slapped Jamie on the shoulder, then poured them each a drink and pushed one across the table to him. He held his mug up, expectant. Jamie raised his to meet his brother's. They clinked. Jamie set his back down on the table.

"Bad luck!" Sid shouted. "Can't cheers and not drink. Bad luck."

Jamie nodded and took a little sip. "I don't really drink much," he said.

"Well," Sid laughed, "I'll make up for you." He downed the rest of his and poured himself another and chuckled to himself for quite a while before stopping. Then they were in silence again, but Sid seemed easier with it, and so was Jamie. Sid drew in deep purposeful breaths, as if to say something, which he just let go—catch and release.

Jamie was on his first glass and Sid his fourth when his brother finally asked, "When'd you get in?"

"This morning."

Sid laughed. "It's afternoon now. You get lost?"

"Went up to the hospital."

"Oh," Sid sneered. "And how is our dear doctor? Our

*angel?*" He leaned back into the sofa.

"Don't."

"Whatever." He finished his drink and poured another. There was no hesitation there. He refilled automatically. Just like their dad had done.

They were quiet again then for a while.

"How long are you staying?" Sid asked. "*Are* you staying?"

"Just for a bit. Or, it was going to be just for a bit, but I talked to the doc, earlier, and...Yeah. I mean, if that's okay. That I stay. But I don't know for how long, anymore."

Sid took a drink. "It's your place as much as mine. Just...just asking."

"Thanks." Jamie drank. He hated it. "Not sure how long. Just until...I don't know. Figuring things out."

Sid nodded. Then he said, "I've got a phone."

"What?"

"A smart phone. And next door, the Lemmonses, they're old and don't lock up their Wi-Fi. So, I watched your fights on YouTube, is what I'm saying. What ones of them are on there. Good quality, some of them. The videos I mean, not the fights. But they're good too. Obviously."

"What did you think? Of the fights I mean, not the videos."

Sid grinned. "Think I could still take you?"

They could fight one hundred times and Sid *might* win once—maybe a lucky punch or a freak injury, like Jamie blowing out his knee or breaking his hand on his brother's forehead—but probably not even then.

"Do you?" Jamie laughed.

Sid smiled the same way as when they were little, defiant. "Did you want to watch them some time? Get a few beers, and—"

"Yeah!" Jamie said. He almost screamed it.

Sid flinched. He took a drink.

"Yeah," Jamie said. "Some time. That would be cool."

After that it was easier, and they spent a good while talking, though Jamie didn't know exactly how long, as he'd had to sell his watch. He told Sid about living in the city and the gym and Mo and Robbie and his fights. Sid didn't ask any questions, at all. It wasn't what Jamie was used to, and it unnerved him a little. Eventually, he said he was tired of talking about fighting. He wasn't—he'd never get tired of it—but he was sure Sid was tired of listening.

"So, how about you?" Jamie asked. He leaned forward. "You okay here? Everything okay?"

"Yeah, fuck. Why d'you keep asking if I'm okay? Why wouldn't I be?"

"No, no reason. I just...I meant work. With work. What do you do?"

Sid had drunk a lot more than Jamie, but he barely showed it. The only thing that gave it away was how he occasionally struggled to pull the right word out of the air. Their dad had done the same thing, drank more and more of his words away until it was only silence or screaming.

"I just do stuff. I'm a . . ." He waved his hand in circles in the air. "An odd-jobber. A handyman, to get technical."

"Really?"

"Yes, really. Why 'really?'"

"I don't know. I'd have thought...the house..."

Sid put his drink down on the table. His shoulders tensed and bunched up under his ears and whatever looseness he'd allowed himself was gone. "Everything in this house is sturdy. Everything works. Everything."

Jamie held his hands up, as if surrendering. "No. I know. I more meant like, how it's the same. It feels the same."

"So?"

"I just thought that, if you could have, you'd have changed it. Made it new."

Sid relaxed back into the sofa and picked his drink back up. Jamie lowered his hands.

"I thought about it. A lot of times. Just, not my decision to make."

"Then whose?"

Sid held eye contact with him, raised his eyebrow.

Jamie looked away, out the window. "Remember how we could tell the time by the light? The way it fell across the wall. When we were kids."

"Hell," Sid said. "It's only you that can't anymore. But speaking of, it's time for me to go, unfortunately." He downed his whisky, slapped his knees, and stood up. Jamie would not have been so sure on his feet after that much drinking. He might not be now, and he'd only had two. The bottle was half empty, and Sid had drunk all but two measures of what was gone—but he seemed fine. Jamie, however, had already noticed a heaviness in his own tongue and something that felt like a longness of his arm.

"Where you going?"

Sid shrugged. "Commitment. Can't shake it."

"Should I . . . ?"

"Come? No."

"No, go. Away."

Sid laughed. "Go? Why would you go? And where?"

Now it was Jamie's turn to draw useless breaths.

Sid clapped him on the arms. "Make yourself at home," he said, then slid his shoes on. "You are home, aren't you?" He smiled and ducked out the door, closing it firmly behind him.

Jamie sat with that idea. Was he? Home? Was that what this place was to him? Had it ever been? He turned back around and faced the inside of the house, empty now as far as he knew except for him and the whisky, which he quickly picked up and pressed into his chest.

He walked the path worn through the carpet on the stairs, which didn't creak. On the first landing, at the back of the house above the kitchen and bathroom, was Sid's room. At least, it used to be Sid's room. He didn't know if it still was. He put a hand on the handle and stood there a while, and then let it go. It didn't feel right to open, his house or not.

Up the second, shorter, flight of stairs, was his old room and then his father's room at the front of the house, looming down over the street. His father's door was closed. He'd gone in there only once as a child.

He opened his own door and musty air tumbled out through it. The room was not exactly the way he'd remembered it being, but it was probably exactly the way it *had* been.

His twin bed was under the window. It had several thin blankets on it, sun bleached. There was his wardrobe that sagged to the side, his little dresser, and the wooden desk his dad had got from who knows where when he'd heard Jamie hadn't been doing his homework. The desk was bare—he had never done the homework, and his dad had never checked. And there was the empty space against the wall where Dex's bed had been.

He held the bottle in his bad hand and reached across his bed to the window, unlatched it, and lifted. It stuck. Probably hadn't been opened in years. But he was still strong, and the window gave in to him and opened on his second attempt. He sat on the bed and a burst of dust enveloped him, got in his nose and mouth. He could taste the years. He took a drink to drown out the dust. He felt tense, kept waiting for the sound of the door slamming, of size twelves pounding up the stairs.

It was the most he'd drunk in years and he didn't really like it, but when Sid had closed the door on him and left him in there alone, it suddenly felt like what he had to do. He sat there breathing dust and drinking as the sun died down outside and the neighbours' back light flashed on. A cat had jumped onto the fence, tripping the motion sensor, and lighting up the old shed their dad had built one weekend, an exercise that had kept him almost sober as long as it had lasted.

Had he known what the doctor would say? Is that why he'd avoided the hospital first thing? Or, alternatively, was that why he had come back here in the first place, so she could tell him that? But even if he suspected what she'd say, she couldn't actually be right about it. She couldn't be. If the doc was right, then that was it for him. Done fighting. Done being the champ. Done being Jamie, even. Not only for a while but forever. And that just could not be true. So as unlikely as it was, she had to be wrong.

He stood up from the bed. His knees were sore. His back was sore. He bent down to stretch and lost his balance, staggering a few steps and bracing himself with a hand against the wall. The hand cried out in protest. He took another drink and went downstairs, his heel skidding down off the bottom step and jarring his knee and back even more when he landed. He'd left the door and window open to change the air in there. It was suffocating.

The shed had no lock and opened smooth and quiet. The neighbours' light flicked back on when he'd stepped out there, so he could see fine. He put the bottle down and started leaning things out of his way. There were a lot of tools. Some spare wood. He kept looking over his shoulder. Dex's things were in there, some of them. Boxes, the bed frame, the mattress wrapped in plastic. Some of his father's things too. His bedside table, for instance. Just touching those things made him feel like a thief.

And then he saw what he was looking for.

When Jamie had been about ten, his father had acquired a load of leather scraps and gone on and on about their high quality. One weekend when it was sunny, he spread it all out in the back garden with a leather punch and made a heavy bag, using their mother's old clothes as the stuffing. A wooden arm hung from the back of the house like gallows, which Sid had clearly replaced one of the supports for in the years gone past—the one beam brighter than the others.

He grabbed it with his good hand, dragged it out, stripped off the plastic, and hoisted it up onto the hook. The bag swung gently on the chain until it slowed and stopped, then the garden went dark. He drank more whisky, spilled some on himself, and waved to get the light back on. When the light hit him this time it felt different. It felt like cage lights. It felt like he was back where he belonged.

He drove his foot into the centre of the bag, sending it flying backwards, straining against the chain. It folded a bit—it was bottom heavy—but it held together fine and the arm seemed sturdy. When it swung back at him, he pivoted out of the way, and the bag flew through his empty space and he caught it on the way past with another kick. When it came back, he pivoted again. Each time the bag returned, he slid out of its way—second nature, even drunk—and kicked it as it passed, until he felt bold.

The next time the bag swung at him, he stayed where he was, put his knee into the middle of it, tried to drive it right through. The bag folded again and stopped swinging, and his knee flared with unexpected pain—it had been a while since he'd done that—and he stumbled a step back, barely keeping his feet under him. He fired a jab. His hands were unwrapped, and he didn't have any gloves on, so he threw the first one light, a test. The bag was soft in the middle, and his wrist felt alright. So he did it again, each new addition to the combo landing a little harder.

Jab. Jab, left hook. Jab, left hook, right kick. Jab, left hook, right kick, left hook. Jab, left hook, right kick, left hook—

Right cross.

He fired the knockout punch by instinct. He'd had too much to drink to fight any other way. The pain shot up his arm into the darkness behind his eyes. He dropped to his knees, grinding them against the dust and stones.

He crawled over, pushed an ashtray out of his way, and sat up against the side of the house. He tried to control his breathing, but it came out all ragged, pulsing, like the engine of a car that wouldn't start. His eyes were hot. He'd only come to check in on Sid for as much time as it took for things to cool down in his hand and back home at the gym. And then he was going to call and get Mo to forgive him and buy him a ticket back. And that was going to be the last time he'd ever have to think about this town, let alone stay in it. That had been the plan. But maybe the doc was right. Maybe that was it for him. Maybe there was nothing to go back for. Maybe. Or at least, maybe it was too early to tell. He'd just got here after all. Maybe he still had it in him, somewhere deep down. People did. He'd heard about the guy who had a brain tumor and then went back to fighting, or at least grappling. Jamie might be fucked up, but was he brain-tumor fucked up? He could still come back. Not now obviously, but maybe.

He picked up the bottle and sat there and didn't move except to drink—not when the light flicked out, not even when the rain came down, ringing off the shed roof like distant applause.

HIS HAND WAS SORE IN the morning, but it was nothing compared to his head.

"You left the shed open."

Sid stood hazy in the doorway. The bottle of whisky, still a third full, stood on the bedroom floor in front of him.

He was curled up on his childhood bed. A damp draft came in from the window behind him, scraping at the exposed skin at the small of his back where his shirt pulled away from his jeans.

"Sorry," he said.

"It was raining."

"Sorry. I don't normally drink. Sorry."

Sid set a mug on the carpet beside the bed. "Get up. Time to go," he said.

Jamie sat up and pulled one of the old blankets, damp, into his chest. Sid shimmered like he stood across a hot, wide highway. His T-shirt hung off him almost like a tent. His hair was wet.

"Sorry. Won't do it again," Jamie said, and looked outside. It was still raining. A corner of plastic reaching out from under the bottom of the now-closed shed door.

"I know. You said already. Now come on. Get up," Sid said, then left.

Jamie choked down a mouthful of the sour coffee, and then another, and then he finished it and closed his eyes and stuck his face out the window into the cool air.

He was still dressed, so he only had to slide his shoes on when he went downstairs. He stepped around his bag, which still leaned against the wall in the entryway, and out the already open door.

"Should I bring my bag?"

Sid screwed up his face. "No," he said, shaking his head, and he walked away.

It was still raining, still windy. Jamie held his mouth open to the sky, hoping to wash the fur from his tongue.

Sid led him down the road in silence toward the edge of town, the same route they used to walk as kids to get to the tracks, but when his legs wanted to take him right, Sid went left down an unfamiliar lane that quickly seemed to become nothing but trees either side, and Jamie followed, just like he used to.

"You ever see Dex around?" Jamie asked.

Sid said nothing, stared at the ground ahead of him.

"I used to see him sometimes," Jamie said, "in the crowds, in the city, when I first got there."

Sid didn't answer. Even as kids they hadn't talked much about Dex beyond whose fault it was. Sid blamed Doctor Carroll. He'd convinced himself that Dex's recovery would be her doing, so he thought his death was too and couldn't be pushed off that idea. The doctor blamed Jamie's father, he knew, even though she never said it out loud. Jamie had also thought it had been their father's fault, because things usually were. But eventually he realized it had been his fault, his and Sid's, though he'd never said anything about that. He wondered if Sid understood that now too, that Dex's blood was as much on their hands as in their veins.

"It wasn't him, obviously," Jamie added.

His brother veered off the road and grabbed a fence post, climbed the wire like a ladder, and dropped down into a field on the other side. Jamie followed. The wires shook as he climbed and flung water off like dogs shaking dry.

Sid climbed easily up the hill that rose in front of them, but Jamie slipped on the rain-slick hill, scraping gouges into the field, falling sometimes to the ground and muddying both knees and his left hand, and trailing increasingly far behind.

"You used to be able to do this," Sid called back.

Jamie scrambled faster after him, gaining ground but getting even dirtier in the process. When he reached the top of the hill, Sid was already descending with ease. The field ended at a low stone wall, on the other side of which was a cemetery.

"Really?" he said, but Sid was too far ahead now to hear. Jamie's footing was unsure, his descent a series of slips and skids and short falls.

He swung a leg over the wall and straddled, collecting himself. He was soaked through and half painted over with mud. And there was a low throbbing behind his eyes and a rot in his stomach. And all just to come to the fucking cemetery.

He'd never been here, but he knew exactly who Sid was trying to show him was buried here, because he knew who wasn't.

"You know he started walking along the coast? He asked me once where we spread the ashes out, and then later he started walking by the sea. Can you believe that? Would you have ever thought?" Sid said.

The gravestones seemed to sag and slouch, angled from the struggle of their weight against the weakness of the wet earth.

Sid had stopped in front of a stone a few rows up that was newer than its neighbours, standing straighter. Jamie hunched his way over to it.

CHARLES EDWARD STUART
1958–2018
Father

Sid's rigid posture, which had carried him from their house, disappeared. He stood slump shouldered, threading his fingers through his thin beard. His gaze darted between the stone and Jamie.

"I didn't know what else to say," he said. "And it's by the letter, the carving rate."

Jamie nodded. *Father.*

The rain stopped, and Sid disappeared, and the writing on the other gravestones and the howling of the wind and the heat in his hand and the colour from the grass all vanished too. And it was just Jamie and this headstone so close to him. Too close. He didn't even think about it, he just brought his knee up and extended his leg and drove his hips forward. It just happened. His foot crashed, toes to the sky, against the top of the stone. He felt it crack.

His foot snapped back to the ground, the muddy print of it stark against the smooth grey stone, the edges spattered outward. The stone was uncracked...but he'd felt something.

He was sure of it.

"What?" Sid whispered.

Jamie barely heard him over the rain. He shook his head. He'd felt something—not in his foot, but through it. But the stone was still in one piece, with no cracks he could see. But it was crooked now, like those at the bottom of the hill. A slight but noticeable lean backwards, a gentle repulsion.

"What the fuck?" Sid said, much louder. He took a heavy step toward Jamie and made as if to square up, then stopped and dropped his head down and slouched back to the low wall. He scissored his legs over it and climbed effortlessly up the hill.

"Wait," Jamie called, and ran after him. At the wall, his foot slipped in the mud and he caught his toes on the top stone and tumbled down on the other side. He reached out, instinctively, with both hands to break his fall, and pain burned up his arm again and he collapsed in a heap. He was sick—a little over himself, but mostly over the mud.

Sid was at the top of the hill already, looking down. "Do you know what that fucking cost me?" he shouted. "Do you? Do you have any fucking idea?"

Jamie scrambled back to his feet and chased his brother up the hill, but Sid was already gone, and Jamie lost his footing and backslid in the mud several more times before making it back to the road.

The door to the house hung open and bounced in the wind. When he leaned against the wall to pull his shoes off, he left a wet imprint of himself on the paint. When he'd stripped off his soaked-through socks, he noticed his bag was gone. He looked back out the door to see if he'd missed it by the garbage cans or on the street. He hoped Sid hadn't thrown it out somewhere—he couldn't afford to replace it. It would make sense though. Sid had invited him in, and that's how Jamie had acted. He'd have kicked himself out. He'd only have himself to blame. But his bag wasn't out there—there was nothing out there but the rain washing trash down along the side of the street.

"It's in your room," Sid said. He'd already changed into dry track pants and a dry T-shirt, though it was wet at the neck from where his hair dripped onto it. When his hair was darker from the rain, it was almost the colour of Jamie's. "And I closed your window."

"Thanks."

Sid turned and went back into the kitchen. He still hadn't looked at him, not directly. Jamie wrung his socks out onto the step and closed the door. He didn't love this house. Didn't even like it. But he might never have felt more relieved in his life than he did standing there, dripping in the doorway, hearing that he wouldn't have to leave it.

"Made you another coffee. Irish-ed it up. Need to, day like today."

"The good stuff," Jamie said, standing with his back to the door, looking into the heart of the house, sending small splashes into the thin carpet as he shed the rain of the morning, limp socks swaying in his hand.

## Age Fourteen

Jamie saw Sid waiting for him across the street the moment he stepped outside, hands in his pockets, eyes closed against the sun. He would have looked peaceful if it wasn't for the ring of skin around his eye swirling with the colours of eggplant and smoke and backyard cider. Jamie didn't think Sid went to class anymore, and he didn't know what he did during the day instead. But he knew he'd always be outside waiting. Jamie would have preferred to be able to go anywhere other than with Sid the day after he caught a beating, but there was nowhere, no clubs or anything after school.

There should have been something, even he knew that, but there was only Sid.

"How's the eye?" Jamie asked. The night before, their father had accused Sid of stealing a fiver from his wallet and they'd fought, for a few seconds at least. And then their father'd turned on the football and made Jamie and Dex watch it with him, and Sid stomped out of the house and didn't come back until the thin hours of the morning.

"S'fine," Sid said, and they waited in silence for Dex.

Jamie might have worn sunglasses to hide the bruise, but Sid wanted people to see.

Soon Dex appeared in the doorway. There was only the one school in town, so they were all together, if they were there at all. He leapt down the stairs and dashed blind across the road toward them. A white van pulled up short and honked its horn, and Dex jumped up into the air and ran and crashed into to Jamie, wrapping his arms around him like a python.

"S'go then," Sid said.

Jamie wedged his arms down between Dex and himself but couldn't pry himself out of his little brother's grip.

"Let me go," he said. "Come on, you know how he can get the day after."

Sid was charcoal. He filtered everything that came from their father before it got to them. But sometimes it was too much for him to handle, and then it passed through him to them, and in those moments Jamie struggled to see where his brother ended and his father began.

Dex let go and brushed his long hair from his face and took off down the street after Sid, leaving Jamie alone to catch up.

Sid was in a better mood than Jamie'd expected, and that lasted until they got close enough to see their father's primer-grey van parked crooked on the street out front. Their dad wouldn't normally have been home, but a few weeks before he'd made them watch him put on a big show of pouring all his booze down the drain and now he kept trying to make them spend all kinds of time with him.

"Fuck that," Sid said, not slowing. He kept on walking. There was a gas station on the edge of town, and Sid angled them toward the door when they eventually reached it.

"I don't want to," Jamie said.

Sometimes his brother would try to convince the clerk to sell him a pack of smokes, saying it was for his father. Sometimes it worked, sometimes not. Either way, he made Jamie and Dex go into the aisles behind him and slip things into their too-big, second-hand coats when the clerk was busy with him.

"It's fine," Sid said.

"No."

Sid spun and inhaled, drove his finger into Jamie's chest. But then he exhaled, whistling almost, and clapped his brother on the shoulder. "I said it's fine."

At the shop door, he stopped and turned and tried to raise his eyebrow to them, but the swelling made that impossible, and it just twitched. Jamie avoided eye contact with the clerk. Sid grabbed them three Cokes.

He dropped them on the counter and pulled a crumpled five from his pocket. He looked at Jamie and smiled, almost embarrassed, and shrugged. His narrow shoulders almost touched his ears. He gave the change to Dex.

They walked single file along the side of the old country roads to avoid any traffic that might be coming through. There wasn't any really, not out there. But that's what their mom had told them to do one morning a long time ago, so that's what they did.

Dex and Jamie drank their Cokes while Sid held his to his eye. They shoved the empty cans into the body of whatever greenery they were passing when they finished.

They cut across a field, and Dex tickled his palms by running them across the tops of the long grass. Sid marched on as if he knew where he was going, Dex dawdled along as if he wasn't going anywhere, and Jamie walked back and forth between them based on who looked most likely to get into trouble. They were alone in those fields except for the bellow of cattle he could never actually see.

Jamie realized where they were going, and then a second later why they were going there. His chest tightened. "Hey," he said. "He's probably gone out by now. We could go home."

Sid squinted at him, his black eye closing all the way and quaking in the attempt to reopen. He shook his head.

Jamie followed him. He didn't want a fight over it.

They ended up on another country lane and walked in silence for a while until it widened to cross the main road out of town, which here was two lanes wide with a handful of houses alongside it. Limp strings of smoke waved up from the chimneys and bent in the wind. Sid crossed without looking, as if he didn't even care if he got hit by a car. He was so fucking cool when he did things like that. He wasn't afraid of a goddamned thing. But Jamie made Dex stop. They waited a second out of principle, for the nothing to pass them by, and then they hurried hand in hand to catch up. Dex kept hold of Jamie's hand until he realized he was doing it, then jerked it away and wiped it on his pants. The road dipped and darkened and narrowed, became unpaved, more a path than anything else. And they walked a hundred metres or so until it rose up in front of them.

*It*, in this case, was the low, stone train-bridge, though trains made much less use of the structure than kids—and the type of older man that likes to go where the kids go—where they threw things at passing cars or smoked and drank and did whatever else they needed something that resembled privacy for.

Or in Sid's case, to put his back to the town and drop his feet one after the other on the half-buried wooden beams of the tracks that measured his progress away from everything, until eventually his empty stomach or his bare arms in the evening air reminded him there was even less ahead of him than there was behind, and he would turn back.

That's what they did now. Sid launched himself out into the world, and Jamie and Dex trailed in his wake, playing games with their footsteps. They tiptoed along the steel rail, arms wide for balance, and when they reached a place where the greenage fell away from beside them, and the track ran along a narrow ridge with a steep bank either side, the wind came in from the coast and hit them and they struggled to stay upright. And Dex would grab Jamie's sweater and more often than not bring them both down.

At one point, Sid stopped, and they stopped too, and they all three stared ahead into the distance, and Sid dropped and placed his ear to the ground.

When he got up, the pale dust and dirt from the ties and ballast striped his black hoodie like he was a convict in an old cartoon.

"Train's coming," he said.

"Wow!" Dex shouted. Though they were on the tracks, train sightings were still a rarity out there.

The thing slithered up over a hill in the distance.

"Play chicken," Sid said, so calmly.

"No," Jamie said, and immediately turned to slide down the short slope into the ditch beside the track, but Dex held on to his sweater, and now Sid held onto Dex's.

"Play chicken, I said."

"Sid...no way, man. Come on."

Sid said nothing back to him, just closed his fist and his swollen eye and snorted.

"Fine," Jamie said. "Just do as he says, Dex." A scare was preferable to a beating. And anyway, if this is what Sid needed, then Jamie would try to give it to him. Their brother didn't really want to put them in danger. He just wanted to feel what it was like to be in control, to have power over someone. They waited while it approached. Dex wrapped his hands around Jamie's thighs, even though the train was a ways off yet. He wrapped his legs around Jamie's leg and buried his face in his side, already starting to pull him off balance.

"It'll be fine," Jamie said. Dex didn't say anything. From down at the base of the embankment, Sid grinned.

The train drew closer, Dex squeezed tighter, and Jamie struggled to take in full breaths. The train straightened out on the tracks in front of them, the dust it kicked up looking like heaving angry smoke—rolling grey clouds of it. It grew as it neared them, and he had to raise his head to see through the windows that were the thing's eyes into the dark empty cab behind them. Jamie felt like it was coming for him specifically, like the whole point of its journey was just to find him there on the tracks, though he knew he'd only actually matter to anyone on it if it was delayed because it hit him. The track rumbled, and his legs were shaking harder than his hands.

"Okay," he said to Dex. It was a ways off still, but Jamie knew Sid would be satisfied with this effort. He tried to step away and nearly fell over across the tracks, unbalanced, legs tangled. If he fell, he didn't know how he'd land, who'd be on top, if Dex would let go or grip harder, or how long it would take him to get them both up.

"Dex, let go!" he shouted. But his little brother only hugged him tighter.

"Dex," he shouted again, and he pressed the palm of his hand into the soft, cold skin of his brother's face and pushed, but Dex had his hands locked together almost like he made a single fist from both of them, and Jamie had never easily broken that grip.

The train had closed that last distance so fast. It was unthinkable.

Sid scrambled up the side of the hill toward them and had almost reached the top when the long, dull wail of the train's horn rang in their bones. Jamie felt it in his teeth. There was someone in the cab now—a man, and he was panicked, and he was close.

Sid froze. His wiry muscles rippled, struggling against themselves. And then Jamie saw his brother for the first time. It wasn't that Sid wasn't scared. It was that Sid was more scared than any of them. Sid's mouth moved as if he was speaking, but Jamie heard nothing but the pleading horn and the rush of blood through his ears.

Jamie tried to drag himself and Dex off the tracks, but almost came down across them again. "Sorry," he said. And he balled up his fist and brought it down into his brother's soft face, which was frozen in fear exactly like Sid's. Dex let his grip slip some, and Jamie hit him again and again and Dex let him go and stumbled back off the tracks, disappearing over the side of the bank.

And then Jamie was moving backwards too, in silent slow motion, watching the space he'd just occupied fill up with the blurred train. He fell, almost weightless, through a moment that lasted as long as any he'd ever had, then he landed on his back at the base of the embankment, and the sky was blank and grey above him. Jamie lay there a moment, listening to the fading whistle of the train down the tracks, and struggling to cough, and weakly wiping the mud of dust and tears from his stinging eyes.

Sid was shouting. "Oh shit, Jamie. Oh shit."

Jamie sat up and struggled against breaths that would only come halfway in. He crawled up the hill, then across the now empty tracks, which were warm when he placed his hands on them, and looked down at Sid, who knelt over Dex, saying "uh" over and over and casting searching glances in every direction, looking for someone to help.

Dex was sprawled out in the dirt, his head on a large rock that was half buried in the dry dirt. His eyes were closed, and he was open-mouthed and breathing shallow like he was sleeping. He didn't stir when Sid shook him, though his head lolled back and forth, leaving thin smears of red on the stone. Out of the ground beside him grew a lone thistle, stem rigid and leaves sharp. But on top, where it flowered, the thousand spikes it showed to the world were a delicate purple, the colour of his mother's favourite rain boots.

# Chapter 3

THE SMOKE DETECTOR SHRIEKED OUT to all corners of the house. He grabbed a tea towel and swung it, driving the smoke away from the machine. It quieted, but he heard shuffling upstairs.

"Already trying to burn the place down?" Sid asked as he descended the stairs.

"Just... making breakfast."

Sid laughed and pretended to box him as he walked past, pumping a series of sloppy, looping body shots that didn't connect at good angles. He slid the window open as wide as it would go. He looked at the pans. "For how many of us? That's a whole pack of sausages."

Jamie forced a laugh. He wasn't used to eating when he didn't have anything to eat for except not dying. "I guess I didn't know how long sausages take. They burned."

Sid turned the burner down. "Not your timing, your temperature."

The eggs had turned a very dark brown at their edges, the yolks hardened through. They ate in the dining room, the little room beside the kitchen where he, Sid, Dex, and their father had gone through the charade of family dinners for the first month after their mom died and they'd had to move in with him. The table and chairs were simple—blocks and squares and rectangles—but sturdy. Their father had made them. They'd last forever, but they wouldn't sell for a cent; there was no art in them.

Jamie had about twice as much food on his plate as Sid did. Even for someone who wasn't an athlete, Sid didn't seem to eat much.

"So, you got a girlfriend?" Sid asked.

Jamie slowly shook his head. "Training always got in the way. Why?"

Sid laughed. "Just wondering how you got to be thirty years old without learning how to cook sausages." He pointed at Jamie with his fork, a little burned sausage on the end. It might still have been raw in the middle; Jamie didn't know how to tell. He thought maybe he should say something, but he didn't want to point out any more of his failures if Sid hadn't already noticed.

Jamie shrugged. "Never had to. Everything's cooked for me during camp to make sure I eat the right stuff, and outside of camp I just have protein shakes for breakfast. And Robbie likes to cook for people. Think it gives him something to do."

"Well, the toast is good."

"You made the toast."

Sid smiled and tore a piece in half with his teeth bared like a wild dog.

There was another shrill peal, though from farther away. It took him a second to recognize it. He didn't hear it much.

"Is that your phone?" Sid asked.

Jamie nodded.

"You gonna get it?"

Jamie took a sip of coffee, looked out the window to the water dripping from the corner of the shed. That call would almost certainly be from Robbie or Mo, and Jamie could not bear to hear the voice of someone he knew was still in the gym, maybe even hear the sounds of people training in the background, while he himself was standing in his childhood home. And after doing that, he didn't know if he'd be able to carry on the talk with Sid, here.

The ringing stopped, and they finished breakfast.

"Can you manage the dishes without flooding the house?" Sid asked, and then he shovelled the last bit of burned sausage into his mouth. He stood, still chewing, and dusted his hands together so hard it sounded like clapping. "Got to go."

"Go? You only got in, like... I don't know. Late." Sid not returning until Jamie was sleeping had happened quite a few times in the week since he'd been back, though admittedly he struggled to stay up past eleven—an affliction left over from needing to be in the gym before anyone else. He wondered if that would ever go away.

"Work," Sid said. He shrugged.

"I thought it was work last night?"

"Who works at night? Nah. Work now. Out with friends last night."

"I haven't been out with a group of guys in a long time. I was always in a training camp, or my friends were, so we just never really did it."

"Huh."

"And then when I had to stop fighting, like, the people I went to stay with, friends and whatever, still had training. And then I started to run out of money, so. Been a long time."

"Sounds crazy," Sid said. He shuffled past him and jogged upstairs.

"So," Jamie said, "sounds fun." Sid must not have heard him, didn't say anything back. Jamie brought the dishes into the kitchen and watched the water swirl down the drain. There'd been a leak under that sink once, and his father had said he'd get to it when the kids were at school. When they came home, they'd found him passed out, head in the cupboard, legs sticking out across the kitchen floor. It had been

Jamie that had made the mistake of laughing, but Sid who'd taken the beating.

Upstairs, he pulled his phone from his bedside table. The table had been his father's, but he'd use it anyway. He'd taken it from the shed the day before and dumped the contents of the drawer straight into the trash. He'd seen later that Sid had dug everything out, but they hadn't talked about it. Breakfast had been his attempt at smoothing over any possible offence.

He had one message. He sat on his bed, tucked his legs up into his chest, took a few deep breaths, dialled, and soon Mo's strangely soft voice rattled from the speaker.

"Hey, Champ. Long time. Where are you, boy? I been hearing things. People say you show up, stay on their couch a little while, then gone. Where'd you go? Come in. Or call. Not good just to disappear. Anyway, I talked to the Performance Energy Technics. The supplements people. Tried to get them to renew. But they don't renew since you don't fight. What can I say to that? No more payments. But when you come back, they'll be there. So I just want you to know. That's the last sponsor, Champ. No more. No one's mad, just...that's it. Until you come back. Also, Robbie. He says he's calling you, over the past few months. Never pick up, never call back. What kind of way is that to act? Come on. Okay, Champ. Okay, boy. Okay."

The message ended, and he hung up and dropped the phone on his bed and sat there. Sid popped his head in.

"Who was it?" he asked.

"Work," Jamie said. "The gym, I mean, about work stuff. But, whatever. What are you doing?"

"Work stuff. What about you?"

"Go up and see the doc."

"Oh, that bitch." Sid shook his head, disappeared from the doorway. "About your hand? Better off going to the butcher."

"Don't say that. But yeah. And about work."

"Work?" his brother shouted, thumping down the stairs. "Not cooking, I hope."

"Don't know, exactly," Jamie said. He wasn't sure if his brother could hear him at this point, but he said it anyway. "But I'm an athlete, you know. I know all about diet and injuries and physio and injuries and strength and conditioning."

"Say hi to Doctor Mengele."

The front door opened and closed.

"I can do lots of things," Jamie said. But he didn't know if it was true. He could definitely do some things though, and he could do them well. As if to prove it to himself, he went out back and pulled the bag from the shed and hung it. He fired a few phantom shots, half-hearted, barely making contact. When the bag swung slowly into him, he caught it, clinched, and then just leaned into it, resting his cheek against the cold leather. It held him up, rocked him gently back and forth.

**ONE OF HIS FEET TAPPED** his rapid heartbeat on the tile beneath his chair in the reception area. Without an appointment, he would have to wait until Doctor Carroll had a minute to squeeze him in. That was fine. He'd arrived just after lunch. It was nearing five. He just felt bad because he'd had to go to the bathroom twice, and when he'd come back, he'd had to ask if Doctor Carroll had come for him. He didn't want to annoy the receptionist. But otherwise he was fine. Honestly. It seemed like he should have been bored, but the days since he'd been home had consisted of almost nothing but lying on his bed and staring out the windows, sitting on the couch and staring out the windows, loading up and then not watching videos of his fights on YouTube, disposing of things from the shed and the recovering them before Sid got back from wherever the fuck he was spending all his time. This, for all its dreadfulness, was at least a more novel location; people walked by, there was less of a sense of dread.

He kept staring at the little plaque with the little golden gloves. Even looking at the gloves made his hands itch, made the energy swell inside him, made him want to slip a pair on and feel the sweat run down his neck, the flat pressure on his knuckles from landing a clean shot. He even wanted the dumb shock in the jaw of a shot he hadn't seen coming. He just wanted to feel alive.

"James, what an unexpected treat," Doctor Carroll said, pulling his attention back to the present. She had the dark of fatigue around her eyes. "I'm so sorry about the wait."

"No, it's fine." He was happy to see her no matter what. It was only Sid and her in town he knew, and Sid was always out, and the house wasn't easy to be in alone.

"Sorry. So sorry." She walked him back to her office, cup of tea in hand. She sat at her desk, and he sat in the blue plastic chair against the wall.

"Seems like you've had a bit of a busy one," he said.

"Still having, but yes. Every day now. Each year we serve a larger catchment area, and with an ever-shrinking budget. It was something of a stroke of luck I was able to see you straight away last week. It was only as I'd ended my lunch early to try and finish up some paperwork. But enough about that. You look nice today. You've shaved."

"Yeah."

"And that's a nice shirt. You look much better than when you came in last, I must say. And how is Sidney?"

"You know him."

"I do indeed."

"He doesn't mean it, you know, what he says."

"Yes, he does, James. He's wrong, I hope you know, but he means it very much." She looked sad then. Unusual for her to look like she was feeling anything at all. He knew she felt things, obviously. She just tried hard to look like she didn't.

He rubbed at a crease in his jeans. He'd got the ironing wrong somehow and now there was a line down the middle of his leg where he didn't think one should be.

"So, how are you today? Feeling as well as you look, I hope." She held the tea tab between two thin fingers and dragged the bag in circles around the cup.

"Yeah. Being down here, not on couches or whatever...I'm starting to feel like I'm recovering." He held up his hand. "Banged it up a bit the night I saw you, but even considering, it's feeling pretty good." He squeezed it into a fist, held it up. "Couldn't really do this a couple weeks ago, so. Not comfortably, anyway. Think I might have a chance at a real recovery. Maybe it's not as bad as —"

"James. I'm sorry, but —"

"But then I also thought that, like, it might be a while even then, you know? I heard what you said. Even best case, this could take a while, and I ought to do something. With my time. Keep busy. Keep afloat, money wise."

She leaned back in her chair. It squeaked.

"And you told me how thin you're stretched here, so I just thought...there's lots of ways I could help, I bet."

She smiled. "Well, James. This is something unexpected, but I am pleased to see you looking beyond fighting."

"I'm not looking beyond it exactly. I'm not closing the door. I'm just, looking to see what's on this side of the door while I'm here. I'm just taking a minute."

"Regardless, it is nice to see. Unfortunately, I am a doctor, not an administrator."

He rubbed again at the crease. Of course it was stupid. He was stupid. "I know. I'm sorry. I shouldn't have come."

"But I am a *very senior* doctor. So of course I can speak with the administrators on your behalf. And in fact, I think there may be something you can help us out with, at least temporarily. Our primary custodian has been off recently dealing with issues regarding his immigration status, and because of that, last week a patient slipped in a pool of urine and dislocated her kneecap, which we now must arrange physiotherapy for—"

"Exact same thing happened to me once, except the urine I mean, so I'm very familiar. With dislocation, I mean."

She smiled. "Unfortunate, but I'm not surprised. What do you think? Will you help us? Clean up our mess, as it were?" She held her cup over what must have been the trash bin behind her desk and dropped the tea bag into it.

He stood up, crossed the distance to the desk, and extended his hand before she'd even stood to meet him, before she'd even had a chance to put her cup down. He almost hit her in the face. They shook. There was leftover heat in her fingers from holding the tea.

"I assume that means yes," she said.

"Yes. It means yes. Yes." He was still shaking. He let go.

"I shall speak with the appropriate people, but I believe this is something I can arrange. If you let me know how to reach you, I shall call you over the weekend in case there are any hiccups. Otherwise, I shall see you Monday at eight."

"Monday. Eight. In the morning? Yes, of course. Morning. Never mind."

She extended her arms again as she had when she'd first laid eyes on him last week, and then pulled them back again and nodded, and smiled and nodded again, and returned to her seat.

He pretended not to hear her say, "And on Monday I shall take another look at your hand," as he closed the door behind him.

**THE DOOR SLAMMED SHUT. HE** woke in the dark, panicked, and almost fell off the couch. He lurched upright and faced the door. The light flicked on.

"What are you doing sitting in the dark?" Sid asked.

"Waiting. For you." Jamie relaxed and lowered his fists, which he'd tucked up under his chin in an act of unconscious self-defence. "Bit strange waking up here still." His lower back hurt. The couch sagged. He'd been waiting a long time for Sid.

"And why're you dressed up like you've had a hot date?"

"Went up to see the doc."

"You fucking pervert. She's like, seventy."

"She's only maybe sixty," Jamie said, but Sid doubled over laughing then, his braying filling the house, and he mimed a series of digging punches to Jamie's stomach.

Jamie's face went red. He could feel it. "That's not what I meant," he said. He pushed past his brother and walked to the kitchen, where he pulled a bottle of champagne from the fridge.

"Well la-di-da, city boy. What've we got here?" Sid asked when he followed him in.

"I bought it."

"You can afford to buy champagne?"

"Not again I can't. Not anymore."

"So what's the special occasion?"

"Got myself a job."

"Hey, great," Sid shouted. He slapped Jamie on the shoulder.

Jamie almost dropped the bottle, panicked, and clapped it against his chest. "It's just a one-off thing. Nothing permanent. But."

Sid got two mugs from the cupboard and set them on the counter. "No fancy glasses, I'm afraid."

Jamie popped the cork and poured a few surges into each of the mugs.

They clinked rims. Sid's mug had a pattern on it like fancy wallpaper. Jamie's said "World's Best Dad."

Sid drank, and his face puckered. He looked into the mug, stuck his tongue out, flicking it through the air like that stray dog that Robbie always used to feed peanut butter sandwiches to out the back door of the gym when he thought no one was looking. "You ever had this before?" he asked.

"Once."

"S'posed to taste like this?"

"I think so."

"And you like it?"

"It's just what you do," Jamie said. He dragged his tongue across his squeaking teeth.

His brother put the mug down on the counter beside Jamie and picked up a bottle of Worthy's from beside the fridge. He never bothered putting it away. Made more sense to keep it to hand. He poured it a bit in Jamie's cup, mixing it into the champagne, and then doing the same with his own. He drank another sip.

"There we go," he said. "This is more like it. This is what *I* do." He held up his mug to cheers again.

Jamie touched mugs with him and took a drink. The burn of the whisky was much harder to bear when paired with the fizziness of the champagne. It burned him twice.

"Yeah, that's good," Sid said. "Not like that weird, girly, metallic, whatever. Anyway, what are you doing? In the job."

"Like I said, it's just to fill my time with."

"Until you're recovered," Sid said, maybe a bit dully; Jamie couldn't tell the tone of voice. Sid grabbed the Worthy's and went back into the living room. He left the champagne behind. Jamie left it too.

"It's physio," he said. "Helping an old lady with her dislocated knee."

"You've come back a regular Superman, I see."

"I mean, it's not dislocated anymore."

"Literally helping an old lady to cross the street!" Sid laughed, stamped his feet on the floor. A bit of his drink sloshed onto the floral-patterned couch and darkened a single petal. "Back in town not even two weeks and already got a big, fancy job." He lowered his eyes. He brushed a thumb along the damp patch in the fabric and stood up. "Just got home, and already great." He looked briefly at a loose photo on the bookshelf and then went to the window, looking out quietly for a few moments, before he turned around as if nothing had happened, as if his mood hadn't dropped out from under him, and he started putting on a posh voice and saying things like "Doctor Jamie, I presume," and "Paging Doctor Jamie" and laughing himself into a puddle.

But later, he stopped laughing and sat across from Jamie and leaned forward, serious. "Good for you, little brother. Really. But watch out up there. Don't trust her."

"Oh, Jesus. She's fine."

Sid stood up again and started walking circles around the couch.

"Is she fine? Is she? Is *Dex* fine?"

"Dex wasn't her fault."

"The hell he wasn't." Sid finished his drink. He reached out to top Jamie up, but Jamie moved his cup out of the way. Sid's mixture was awful. His brother held the whisky in his hand, looked back and forth between their cups, then filled his slowly, but not as full as before.

"Why the hell wouldn't I trust her? She's a *doctor.*"

"You think I don't know you sent money up there?" He gestured more and more wildly as he talked. "And now you got nothing, and they got e*x*-presso machines or whatever. And you don't think you got played?"

He had sent money up there, but it hadn't been like that. Kage Killers gave out one knockout bonus per card, and he usually won it. Ten grand when he knocked out McCleary to win the title. But he couldn't take money for that. Not after

Dex. He passed it along. He knew hospital equipment was expensive, but he hoped it would add up over time.

"I don't have nothing," Jamie said.

"Yeah?" Sid asked. "Then what are you doing here? Hey?"

Jamie sat back down. He opened his mouth. He didn't have anywhere else to go. But he couldn't say it.

"What did you come back here for if you had anywhere else to go? Anywhere else at all in the entire fucking world?" He was almost shouting. He finished his drink and tossed the mug across the room. It landed with a dull thud on the rug and bounced to a stop against the wall. It didn't look like it broke. "Why'd you come back, hey? Not for Dad's funeral obviously. You know he was doing real good for a while? Had a bit of work, wasn't drinking or nothing. Me neither. Then one day everything went to shit again. I don't know. But now you come back, and you think you were right about him all along."

Jamie sat on the couch. Sid circled him, again, three times while he ranted. He stopped in front of him, leaned down over him like to scare him.

But Jamie had long since had every ounce of fear of men beaten out of him.

Sid pulled the mug from Jamie's hands. Jamie let him. Sid slammed it down in one, tossed that mug on the floor too. It came to rest with a clink against the first.

"So what have you got besides nothing, little brother? What have you got?"

"I've . . ." Jamie started, but trailed off, staring out the window to find anything that would let him change the subject, but there was nothing, there was just them. "I've got to go to bed." He stood up, and Sid took a step back. Jamie climbed the stairs, and Sid stood in the doorway to the living room.

"Fucking *ex*-presso machines," Sid said.

Jamie closed the door to his room and lay down on his bed. Moments later, he heard the front door close. He connected to the Lemmonses' Wi-Fi and watched some of his old fights, trying to feel once again the confidence of movement, the surety of purpose, the pure simple joy. The absolute, perfect emptiness of mind. He did not find it. His childhood mattress squeaked underneath him as he involuntarily twitched his shoulders and hips in time with his movements in the video. He could not stop feeling where he was. But later, he fell asleep, smiling, with the breeze against his back and a pale blue light in his face, his phone open to a webpage about knee-strengthening exercises.

## Age Fourteen-and-a-Half

Their father placed one hand on the edge of the table at the side of the room, which was covered in pamphlets and papers about cancer and pregnancy and vaccines, and flipped it over. Jamie squeezed his eyes shut against the noise of it landing on the floor. When he opened them, his father was gone, the sound of footsteps disappearing down the hallway. The pamphlets and papers settled gently onto the floor like first snow.

The bottom half of the window was painted over for privacy. Sid walked over to it to try to watch their father walk off through chips in the paint. He was not tall enough to see over. Jamie righted the table and knelt to collect the pamphlets from the floor. Doctor Carroll kept telling them not to fuss about it and offering cups of tea.

Their father'd started drinking again when Dex had gone into hospital and had barely stopped to breathe since. Jamie was surprised he'd even made it to the hospital.

The doctor and Jamie picked the pamphlets up and pushed them in a loose pile on the table, then she returned to her seat opposite them, smoothing her tweed skirt as she sat.

"Should we do this another time?" she asked. "When your father is more... composed?"

"Now's fine," Sid said. He retook his seat.

Doctor Carroll adjusted her glasses. "Because, it may not be appropriate without..."

"He won't come back," Jamie said. He sat beside Sid, a collection of pamphlets still in his hand.

The pregnancy pamphlet had a picture of a woman holding her belly, one hand on top of it and one on the bottom. In the picture Jamie had seen of his mom when she was pregnant, she'd held it with her hands more at the sides. He wondered if that had made any difference, if it changed anything.

A man appeared at the office door. His hair was slicked back. Doctor Carroll shook her head, and the man left.

"You know, I can call someone," she said.

"It's fine," Sid said. "And you said Dex would be fine too, right?"

"No, Sidney. Unfortunately, I did not say that. I said that, *if* he wakes up, victims of traumatic brain injury of his age tend to recover quite well long term. Even complete independence is not out of the question. But there will be difficulties. Many of them."

"Complete independence," Sid said, and he leaned over and slapped Jamie on the thigh. "How about that? Ha."

"What kind of... difficulties?" Jamie asked. The vaccine pamphlet had three different images on it: a happy baby, a happy child, an adult woman drawing a needle.

"Well, anger management is a big one."

Sid snorted. "Probably would have been anyway."

"What do you mean?" Jamie asked the doctor.

"Well, if the patient—" the doctor started.

"Dex," Sid said.

"If Dex wakes up, he will soon find himself in a situation where he's unable to perform a task in the same manner that he was previously able. Eating, for instance."

Sid stood up and walked back over to the window, cocking his head from side to side at the edges of it, trying still to see through the cracks.

"Fine motor skills are often one of the most obvious losses. This often causes significant frustration and violent outbursts, though these may subside some as he learns to adapt."

Jamie nodded to the doctor then retrieved his brother from the window, grabbing him gently by the wrist and leading him back to his chair. "You've got to listen," he said.

"I'm listening," Sid said. "He'll adapt."

Cancer pamphlets were the most numerous. Some had drawings of skin or brains. A few had men leaning solemnly against a fence, but most were pink, had see-through drawings of breasts or reproductive organs. He'd seen those ones before. A lot of them. He piled them all up and shoved them underneath the others as best he could, so they were out of view.

"I want to caution you about being too optimistic. He may suffer from headaches, dizziness, ringing in the ears, difficulty sleeping, memory problems, a whole host of things. His struggle will be tremendous, and that is if—"

"He's a tough kid," Sid said.

"And I hate to say this to you boys, but I must—that's *if* he leaves at all; he hit his head badly when he fell. And there are additional dangers associated with long hospital stays."

"He's a tough kid," Sid said. "He's a Stuart, huh? That's good for something." He stood up again and nodded at the doctor and walked out.

The doctor stood up, smoothed her skirt again, and walked across to sit beside Jamie.

Out in the hallway, there was a loud beeping and the squeal of many shoes on the floor. It wouldn't have anything to do with Dex or Sid, but he held his breath anyway and refused to look out to whatever was causing that panic. He just sat there, with the doctor.

"Are you okay?" she asked. "At home?"

Jamie smiled and nodded. It was how he always answered that question.

"Well, I think I might get someone to check in," she said, and then, perhaps sensing him tense, added, "just to make sure you have the resources to deal with this."

Jamie nodded, because he didn't think arguing would get him anywhere. She put her hand on his shoulder, and then the two of them looked at the floor and listened to the quieting beeps and squeak of shoes on the floor outside her office.

And then Sid's silhouette appeared in the window and he rattled his knuckles against the glass and shouted something Jamie couldn't understand.

**THEY WALKED TO THE BEACH** in The Shade, which is what everyone called the part of town on the other side of the headland, because the ridge the hospital was on made the sun set earlier on this side than the other. The only beach they ever normally went to was the lonely one a long march out of town their dad dragged them to for wrestling. So, though he knew they should be back with Dex, Jamie felt a bit excited as they headed down to the crashing waves. Sid walked quiet like he always did. Jamie was quiet most of the time now too.

The stones on the beach were little grey ovals, and Sid started throwing them at the sea—not to skip, but to pierce. Jamie threw some too, but eventually he just sat down and watched. His brother picked up the stones and bounced them once or twice in his hand as if to measure the weight. Then he lurched forward and whipped his torso—which seemed to have no bones in it at all when he moved like that—and slung his arm over and forward, hurling the rock out into the surf. His back foot extended behind for balance, like a dancer.

The damp of the beach stones soaked through Jamie's jeans, and he stood back up and tugged them away from his clammy skin.

Sid saw him. "You getting undressed?" he asked.

"What?"

"You going to go in the water? If you're going in, I'm going in," Sid said, and he pulled his shirts over his head in one motion and threw them on the ground. His chest was purple and yellow with the broad, aging bruises he'd taken when their father found out Dex had been hurt, only a few spots of healthy pink shining through. Seconds ago, he'd looked boneless and loose, but now that his shirt was off, he looked like he was all bones, nothing but bones, pressing out from through too-tight, too-thin skin.

"Let's go in," he said, "like we used to."

"We never used to."

"Come on," he said again, and he bent, pulling his shoes off amid a series of small, sideways hops. He smiled. "Like we used to."

"Sure. Like we used to."

Sid breathed and rubbed his hand over his hair. He slid his jeans down and kicked them away from the water and then ran out into the sea, blue boxer shorts and marbled skin, taking five, six, seven steps in before being run over by an incoming wave.

He stood up shivering, arms already wrapped around his chest, teeth chattering. "Come on," he urged.

Jamie kicked his shoes off, rolled his jeans up to his knees, and then walked a few ginger steps into the biting water. Sid saw this and crashed out farther, half swimming half scrambling. Jamie stayed where he was, kicking the foam on top of the water, while one brother lay above him in the hospital, and the other was sinking farther and farther away from him into the cold below and shouting for him to come and join.

# Chapter 4

**HE HADN'T SLEPT. BUT THEN,** he'd never been able to sleep before a fight, either. Big days, both. He'd just lain in bed and worried. Not about *how* he'd lose, although he sometimes did slip into thinking about the practicalities of defeat despite Mo's urging him not to. But about what losing would mean. The knock-on effects of it. At the gym he had felt three things. The first, that this was the only place that stood between Jamie and coming home with his tail between his legs. The second, that he didn't really belong there, and that it was only the fact that he kept finding a way to win that caused them to overlook that—they tolerated him due to his success. And the third, a truth that emerged over time, was that fighting was who he was, more than what he did. To lose was to *be* a loser. All this had been proven true since his defeat, in the end, so in hindsight he felt his worries valid despite all Mo and Robbie's urging across the years that they weren't. Those were some of the things he worried about, the specific ones that he could articulate, the one or two times he'd ever actually managed to articulate them. But there were other fears too, older ones he couldn't articulate at all, which grew from watching his father mark a wrestling ring in beach sand with his toe, and what inevitably happened when Jamie lost.

If he occasionally drifted off to sleep through all that, he'd wake soon after, arms jerking up to strike or defend. It should have affected him in the ring—the anxiety and exhaustion—but the adrenaline always carried him through.

This last night had mostly been reading and rereading articles on knee injuries until his phone battery died, and then charging it, and in the meantime taking up the notes he'd written over the weekend and rereading those—though a lot of that time was spent just deciphering them. His writing was poor and confused even when he *could* hold a pen for more than a few minutes without his hand aching so bad he had to hang it out the window to cool it off.

And when he wasn't doing either of those things he was looking over into the dark across the room and remembering how Dex had always seemed to already be looking at him whenever he looked over. At first, Jamie had worried that being back in town would mean too many memories of his brother, but now he wished there were more. Most time he spent with Dex had been in the fields, on the tracks, at school. He didn't go to those places anymore, so he was rarely reminded. And now that side of the room was empty. Sid had helped him move the furniture out when they were young and it was too hard to look at.

Only when the sun rose did Jamie actually get up. He didn't want to disturb Sid. His brother had only come back at strange hours for short periods of time that weekend, and they hadn't talked much. Sid had seemed punchy, unfocused. But Jamie'd heard him come in a few hours earlier and stay in, and he was almost certainly asleep now.

The bathroom was a small square with old fixtures—except for the shower, which when he'd been a kid was a rattling tower of thin pipes that dribbled limp streams of warm water down. He was pleased to see that Sid appeared to have made at least one exception to his decision to leave the house a museum and installed a reasonable shower.

Jamie had a toothbrush, the end of a stick of deodorant, and a towel. He'd used up everything else since he'd left the gym and had "borrowed" as needed from whoever he'd been staying with. Since he'd been back home, he'd used his brother's supplies sparingly—he'd washed his hair only once, to get the road off him when he first arrived—so that he was as little a burden as possible.

He didn't want to take any chances today of making a bad first impression—he didn't know how many times he was going to have to walk through the hospital doors before it wouldn't feel like the first time. Or how many times he'd walk through there in total before he headed back to the city for good.

He didn't own a comb. Neither did Sid. He parted his hair for the first time since school photos by scratching a line down his scalp with his fingernails. Then he clipped the fingernails off. He'd ironed his clothes the night before, but he didn't like the look of them in the morning light, so he brought them down to the living room and pulled the iron and ironing board out of the hall closet and did them over while he drank several cups of coffee, padding back and forth between the kitchen and living room in his underwear, flexing at the version of himself reflected in the still-steamy mirror in the bathroom. Through the distance and the steam, he almost looked like himself.

He dressed and tied his one tie, and then retied and retied it, and eventually watched instructional videos on his phone. In the rare event that he'd had to dress nicely—expectations were pretty low for people like him—Robbie had helped him. Robbie couldn't ever explain the process without confusing himself, but if he was just left to do it, his hands would get it done on their own, with no help from his muddy brain. Jamie'd had a jacket once, too—a nice one—but he didn't know where it was anymore.

He scooped a spoon of coffee granules into a clean mug and left it beside the kettle for Sid. Wasn't much, but it was something.

It was barely half past seven when he arrived at the hospital. He walked to the edge of the hill and looked down over the sea, walked across the hospital property to look down on the beach in The Shade, where he and Sid had once spent a notable afternoon. That was where the town's only beach was, but it was barely accurate to call it that.

He took his notes from his pocket, read them over, chased a loose page across the lawn. He walked inside at five to eight. He nodded and smiled at the receptionist. Doctor Carroll was waiting for him just inside the door. "My god, James. And you really are all grown up." She touched him on the shoulder, pressed the back of her hand against her eye. "Come with me and you can get started. Would you like a cup of coffee first?"

"I have already had...a lot."

She led him down a corridor. "You do look handsome, James. Very professional. I'm so pleased. I worried that you would feel it was beneath you." She led him down another one.

"Nah, this seems like exactly what I need. Really."

"Wonderful. Though you will have to change your lovely clothes, I'm afraid. Policy. In any case, it would be a pity to spoil that shirt."

"Don't see how I'd spoil it, but sure."

Down the next corridor, a short, middle-aged man with a moustache stood in front of an unlabelled door with his hands folded at his belly. He wore what looked like grey scrubs. When they reached him, Doctor Carroll said, "James, this is Ivan, who will be showing you around today. Ivan, James."

Ivan opened the door. It was large, for a closet. Densely packed, but well organized. One corner looked like a kind of open shower, but only half as high as it should have been. The walls to the sides were covered by wire shelves, each labelled and orderly, packed top to bottom with cleaning supplies. The far wall was a collection of mops and brooms.

Jamie turned his back to it, looked at the doctor. "Where's...the lady?" he mumbled.

Her normally tightly pressed lips sagged. "Oh dear," she said. "Ivan, if you will excuse us for just a moment." She grabbed his wrist. Her fingers barely circled it, but her grip was strong. Once, Mo's old Brazilian friend came through the gym for a seminar and rolled with Jamie. If anyone who walked through the gym door was stronger than Jamie, it was not by much. But when Thiago wrapped his wrinkly old hand around Jamie's wrist, it didn't come off, no matter what Jamie did. Doctor Carroll grabbed him like that, dragging him to her office with a strength and speed he hadn't known she was capable of.

"Wait right here," she said. She closed the door.

He sat in the blue chair in the office alone, pressed his fists into his cheeks to try and drive the blood out. He was hot, and he felt his heartbeat in his ears and all he could smell from anywhere was bleach and it stung at his eyes.

She had a series of posters behind her desk. A drawing of a half-empty glass of water said, "Regularly drinking water helps to maintain a healthy lifestyle." Another, a drawing of a hand holding pills said, "Unfortunately, no amount of antibiotics will get rid of your cold."

Doctor Carroll returned shortly with two cups of coffee, placed them on the table beside him. She sat in the nearest office chair and rolled it over to him. She nudged the cup of coffee to him. It scraped against the table.

"Here. It's excellent. It's from a...I don't know the actual name—pod machine."

He kept his hands pressed against his face, palms covering his eyes, fingers scratching at his hairline as if trying to peel off the clown mask that was now his face.

"I fear there's been a terrible misunderstanding," she said. "You had thought I had asked you to assist with the physiotherapy."

"But you wanted me to mop up piss."

"Well, no, I didn't want you to 'mop up piss,' as you put it, I only wanted to get you work if you needed it."

"I was a world champion." He took his hands from his eyes, so he could look at her, but she was blurry, and he realized instantly that this had been a mistake. She reached for his hand, but he shoved it down into his lap.

"I know, James."

"And I know all about fucking ACL sprains."

She nodded.

"I've had three and helped, like, five other guys in the gym get through 'em."

"I'm sure you are completely capable, James, but you are not *qualified*, and in a hospital environment—"

"I was a world champion," he said, digging his notes from his pocket. "That's gotta count for something."

"Yes, however—"

"Dislocation of the patella occurs when it is forced from the femoral groove. Surrounding cartilage and soft tissues may also take damage."

"Yes, though—".

"Hamstring and calf stretches. Static and walking half lunges. Passive knee extensions." He let his notes go and they landed on the floor between them. He didn't need them. "Avoid full knee extensions with heavy weight. Half squats, from sitting to standing, gradually lowering the height of the chair. Heel raises. Light elliptical."

She bent down and retrieved the notes from the floor and extended them to him. When he didn't move to take them, she looked at them. She put her glasses on. She squinted at them, and then he was ashamed of his writing like he was everything else. But whether she could read them or not, they were right. He knew that. She made small movements with her ankles, rolling her chair ever so slightly back and forth. She'd folded her hands into her own lap, except when she used the meat of her thumb to dab under her eye.

"I've no doubts about your capabilities. If this is something you would like to pursue, then I would be honoured to help you. Your previous career may even be of use in getting you enrolled in a program somewhere. But at the moment, you are simply not qualified."

He shook his head.

"Do you see? Perfectly capable, yes, but not qualified unfortunately."

"Whatever," he said, standing. "Enjoy your coffee."

"Oh no, James. Please don't leave so upset. I'm so sorry about the misunderstanding. It's all about pieces of paper, do you see? It's only paper. They may not mean anything, but they are still unfortunately very important."

He opened the door and she apologized again, saying, "I'm so sorry, James."

"I'm Jamie. See? Jamie. Not James. And I was a champion."

He closed the door. His nose stung with the scent of bleach and his eyes stung, and he kept his gaze fixed right on his feet, unable to make eye contact with the receptionist as he walked out, measuring one foot purposefully in front of the other so as not to embarrass himself even more by running out like a child fleeing a bully on the playground, reaching tear-blind for the blurry shape of his mother.

A run of the distance between the hospital and the bar, three kilometres, maybe—not as the crow flies, but on roads that folded back and forth overtop themselves as they rolled down the hillside—shouldn't have even left him breathing heavy. He'd have to get his shit together if he was serious about making a comeback, stop dreaming that there might be anything for him outside the cage.

The bar was much the same inside. It was the same woman behind the bar, the same old men sidled up to it.

"Still don't have any milk, I'm afraid," she said.

"Come in for that fancy Japanese whisky?" said Paul.

"Fuck off, Paul," Jamie said. A couple people laughed, Colin especially, and then got very quiet. "Worthy's please. And then another." He still couldn't remember her name. When she looked at him, he was sure that she remembered him, but he felt he'd missed the time when it would have been acceptable to ask.

"Alright," she said, and she poured him his first drink in a tall, narrow glass, the small measure of whisky at the bottom looking like nothing at all against its area. "We celebrating or commiserating?"

He swallowed it and coughed into the crook of his elbow, leaving a whisky imprint of his mouth on the fabric. So much for his nice shirt. He shot a look over at Paul, who stayed quiet.

She poured him his second one. He let it sit in the glass.

"Could have used you on the weekend," she said.

"Why's that?"

"Couple of the guys came in after a good haul, first in quite a while, and bought round after round and gave Paul here a break from picking up the tab. But they got a bit too carried away. Almost had to call the police, not that there'd be any at that time of night."

"You think they would have listened to me?"

"Probably not, to be honest, but you've kept Paul quiet for five minutes since you came in, which is a new record." She laughed, and the men laughed with her, Colin loudest of all.

Jamie rubbed at the crease in his jeans which he'd ironed out three separate times, but he still felt it there. What had she said about Paul picking up the tab? How could a guy that stupid be rich enough to pay for everyone else? And why would someone who was that big an asshole even bother? She'd only mentioned it in passing, but it picked at him.

"I don't know how long I'll be in town, unfortunately. Thinking about going back up to the city sooner rather than later. Should take the comeback seriously."

"I expected so. I was only kidding, really. I mean, this isn't the kind of work I'd have thought you'd be into. Seems a bit beneath you."

He finished his drink. He patted his nearly empty pocket. "Well, I might stick around a while," he said.

"Really?" She brushed a few stray curls behind her ear.

"Yeah. You know, I used to do this on weekends when I was first starting out." He tried to take a drink, but his glass was somehow empty. She filled it again and gave him a wink. He raised his glass and nodded and struck his tooth on the rim of the glass. He didn't feel it; his upper central and lateral incisors were fake, the real ones having been sent tumbling like dice across the canvas in the gym some years before. He'd been too hot and dehydrated after a long summer day in the ring, and his mouthguard felt like it filled his whole mouth and was choking him, so he left it in the corner in between rounds to breathe better and ate a shin to the lips which knocked his teeth from his mouth in a spray of spit and blood.

"You could again..."

"I'll drop in before to double check, but yeah, I'll see you Friday night?"

She smiled at him. She waved, her hand arching backwards through the air. "See you then, Jim. Champ, I mean."

He squinted at her and nodded. No one had called him Jim since school.

**LATE AFTERNOON, AND JAMIE KNELT** beside the two-level coffee table in the living room, nudging things out of the way with the back of a finger like he was investigating a crime scene. There was a remote control for a television that wasn't in the room. A bag from a takeout filled with other takeout bags and cartons. A full ashtray and two empty packs of smokes, tops splayed open like broken jaws and foil packaging half vomited out. And prescription pill bottles, all of them for different medications, many he recognized and some he didn't, most out of date, and all for different people. He looked for some of the painkillers he was used to, the ones he got after surgeries, but there was nothing.

Sid's door shut and Jamie got up from where he'd been snooping. The lights were off, he realized, the curtains drawn. He hadn't noticed. It felt dark.

Sid came downstairs, driving his sharp knuckle bones into his eyes. "Home so soon?"

Jamie held up the bottle of Worthy's he'd bought on the walk home.

Sid nodded, understanding. "So, how was the coffee?"

"Fancy."

"Thought so."

Jamie lay down on the couch, rolled over into the fetal position. "You were right, alright? The job was bullshit. Go get a glass."

"Well, look who knows what's up after all."

Sid got a glass from the kitchen and dropped onto the floor in front of Jamie. He held his glass up and Jamie filled it up and didn't spill all that much, and a lot of what he did spill Sid sucked from the bones of his hand and arm with a laugh.

"So what are you going to do?"

"Don't know. I got a couple shifts at the Anchor for now."

"I'm banned there."

"I know."

Jamie lay on the couch, and Sid on the floor below him. Jamie looked at the ceiling; one time he'd been up late watching TV and his father had walked in the door and met him in the hallway and laid him out without saying a word. He'd just lain there staring at the ceiling for a long time until he heard furtive snores coming from the room above him and got up and went to bed himself. The ceiling looked the same. It would, obviously, but a part of him kept expecting things to be different—almost as much as he kept expecting them to be the same.

"I got something we could do," Sid said.

"What's that?" Jamie said, skeptical, and then guilty because Sid hadn't actually done anything to deserve his skepticism, that he knew of.

"The house. First thing out of your mouth was that it was the same. We can do something about it. Renovate. Remodel."

Jamie must have thought about tearing that house down around him a thousand times, but when he'd returned, he'd found Sid had done basically the opposite and reinforced it so it would stand forever in memory, a mausoleum. But now he was inviting him to throw it all away and start over. He was offering the chance to look into a room without remembering everything that had ever happened there, to destroy what his father had built. He didn't know why Sid changed his mind, but he was happy he had. Though, he quickly felt overwhelmed by how big and unfamiliar the job seemed.

"I don't know how to do any of that."

"I do. And you're strong, aren't you? And you've definitely got the time."

"I do, but I also don't have the money. Like, barely any now, after the Worthy's. My sponsorships died out a while ago now, and travelling... Isn't this type of thing expensive?"

"It won't actually be that bad. Labour'll be free, and I can get materials for cheap."

Jamie sat up. "Okay."

Sid jumped to his feet. He clapped Jamie on the shoulders and shook him, laughing.

"Just until I go," Jamie added. "Until I head back to the city, for my comeback."

"Sure, sure, of course," Sid said quickly, as if he wasn't listening. He poured himself another drink, and the same for Jamie, and he clinked his glass against Jamie's then downed it, refilled it, and headed toward the back of the house.

Jamie sat on the couch and sipped whisky, which didn't taste near as bad as it had only days before—though he was in no hurry to mix in any champagne. "When it's time for me to go back, then it's time. I'll have to go," he said, raising his voice some, as he didn't know where Sid had gone. There was no response.

Eventually, Sid returned with a sledgehammer and crowbars. "For inspiration," he said. "You got any ideas about what you want to do?"

Jamie looked around at the house his father had inherited from his grandfather. "Burn it?" He forced a little laugh.

"Not sure how much that would improve the property value. Why don't I come up with something?" He leaned the hammer and bars up against the side of the couch, sat, and slapped his hand on Jamie's knee, which sent a quick pulse of pain through the joint.

"Jesus," Sid said. He smacked it again. "Like fucking steel." He took his hand back, refilled his drink. "So everything's good here, with the house. Like, it's sound. Say what you will about Dad—"

"One day I might."

Sid's jaw clenched and his eyes snapped shut a second, but then he smiled and exhaled and continued on. "But he was good with tools. And the same for me. So, we don't need to *fix* anything. It's all in good working order. So this will mostly be cosmetic. We may want to redo the flooring—new carpet, or if there's good hardwood down there...maybe knock out a couple walls. That's what everyone's into now: open plan. So maybe knock that one out and then that one and that one. That one's load bearing, so a part of it would have to stay. But I think it would work. What do you think?"

"You'd know better than me."

Sid clapped. "I do. Fucking brilliant. Won't cost too much, with my brains and your brawn."

"When should we start?"

"Well," Sid said, throwing his hands up in the air. "No time like the present."

"Shouldn't we wait? In case we change our minds, or something?"

"You going to change your mind?"

Jamie took a drink.

Sid added, "And I want to see you swing that hammer."

Jamie smiled, stood up from the couch, wrapped his hand around the smooth wooden handle, and felt the satisfying weight of it. It would feel so good to swing. He knew all about swinging hammers. It was a part of his strength and conditioning program. He'd had hundreds of reps of beating a sledgehammer down onto a tractor tire in the alley behind the gym.

Sid pulled out his phone. "Shit," he said. "I was gonna video you knocking a hole in that wall, but I've got to head out." He shot off the couch and up the stairs.

Jamie relaxed his grip and the hammer slid slowly down until the head thudded onto the floor. He slid his free hand across the wall.

Sid came down with his heels skidding madly off the edges of the stairs. "We got time for one though," he said.

"Where do I hit it?"

Sid walked over and knocked on the wall and listened to the sound. "Do you want it easy or hard?"

"What do you think?"

"Here then. This is a stud. Normally we'd strip the drywall, pull out the insulation, and then saw out the studs. But this is just for fun. And you probably won't do too much damage anyway. Shit's strong. This is just, uh, ceremonial. Like breaking a bottle on a boat."

"As if you'd break a bottle like that," Jamie said.

Sid laughed. "I've broken loads of bottles in my time. I just made sure they were empty first." Sid stepped out of the way and reached into his pocket for his phone.

Jamie hefted the hammer back up and practised landing it where Sid had told him. He wasn't worried about the wall hitting back, so he wound up big, like he was back in that alley. He drove his weight forward and arched the hammer over his head. His hand was strong enough to hold it, and even swing it, but the jolt of the impact knocked the hammer loose from his grip.

There was the sound of a blast of thunder, and Jamie looked to the wall where the head of the hammer had forced itself through. The stud was splintered and bent away from him. Jamie imagined it poked out the other side, like a broken bone through skin. The hammer was wedged in, the handle hanging out into the room like an off switch.

"I didn't even have my camera ready," Sid said. He came over and looked at the wall and then his brother. He touched his hand to the hammer, pushed it, and shook his head.

"Where are you going? What are you doing?" Jamie asked.

"Going to meet a friend for a thing."

"I could come."

"Sorry, not that kind of thing," he said, and he left, still shaking his head as the door closed behind him.

Jamie sat down on the floor underneath the hole, the handle of the hammer sticking out above him, running his tongue back and forth across his fake teeth, feeling it all in the flesh and none in the bone.

## Age Fifteen

He'd grown happy to see Sid waiting for him after school, leaning on the wall across the road. When Dex had gotten hurt, everyone looked at Jamie with pity. He hadn't liked that, but he could handle it. But when Dex got pneumonia and MRSA at almost the same time in the hospital and died, people stopped looking at him altogether. That was harder to handle. His brother actively looking for him, at him, was something Jamie needed.

Sid had given up on the pretense of going to school. Jamie didn't know where he went, what he did, or who with, and they never talked about it. But he seemed happier and sometimes had a bit of money. Jamie often smelled the whisky on him now, and he'd started to associate that smell as much with Sid as with their father.

Sid headed out of town with a purpose, but Jamie hesitated. Something felt different about the way he walked.

"Want to go see the doc?" Jamie asked.

Sid spit. "Why the fuck would we do that? She said she was going to help and then she didn't do shit, just like everybody else."

"She's nice. She makes us tea."

"Fuck tea. She's not Mom, alright. And nobody's nice. Not really." Sid kept walking. "You just haven't figured out what she's pretending to be nice for."

Jamie hurried to catch up.

Sid pulled a flask from his pocket and took a quick pull, hiding it behind the collar of their father's old jacket. They hurried out into the quiet country, Jamie occasionally tossing glances to the empty, sun-dappled road behind him. There was no smell of bleach or tea or the sound of squeaking rubber which he'd come to find comforting. It was just whisky on the wind, and it was quiet like the dead.

And soon they were back at the arch, back on the tracks. It seemed like the only place they went anymore. Sid couldn't seem to stop coming back, and Jamie had even fewer options now than he had before. And since Sid had picked fights with everyone else they'd run into out there, they were now just about the only two who ever did. Sid pulled again from the flask, defiantly out in the open now that there was no one around.

"Want to go to the old quarry instead?" Jamie said.

"Why you always trying to get out of this lately? You want to go see the doc; you want to go to the quarry. Grow some balls."

"It's just I went there with Erin last week. It was good."

"Quarry's for pussies," Sid said. He smirked at Jamie, held his gaze.

Even as insulting as it was meant to be, Jamie still appreciated the eye contact. "Haven't talked to her since," he said.

"Huh."

"Her dad won't let me over."

In the wake of the accident, a chain-link fence appeared along the rail bridge area, but by the first time Sid had brought Jamie back, someone had already cut the fence open bottom to top, so it just hung there, curled open like useless curtains.

Sid slipped the flask into his back pocket and threw his coat down the side of the track. He squinted, all cheekbones, into the light.

"Come on," he said. He peeled the shirt from his back, breaking eye contact only when the fabric pulled up over his face. "Come on," he said again, pleadingly.

There were more bruises on his torso than there had ever been before. Some were from their father, certainly, but not all of them. There were others that popped up even when

Jamie knew their father hadn't been home in a few days. And some, though not many, were from Jamie himself, from Sid's "sessions." There were more of them than ever, but he wore them differently now. His skin was ribbons of plum on plague yellow, but he puffed his chest out proudly, shining back at the sun. Most of these were bruises that he had sought out, and that made all the difference.

"Come on," he pleaded again, and he nodded and waved his hand toward himself. He was smiling, and he plucked the flask from his pocket and took another short swig. "Come on," he said, his voice coarsened by the cheap spirit. He turned away now, his spine showing through his thin skin as he made his way down the tracks a little ways.

He turned around and saw that Jamie hadn't moved. "Fine," he hissed. "Go home."

Jamie looked down the hill to the empty road that would lead him back home, to their dad. It would probably be too late to catch the doctor now. He kicked at some of the ballast stones from in between the ties and pulled off his coat.

Sid smiled. The sun was coming down hard on them, but it was the brightness of Sid's grin that made Jamie look away. He pulled his hoodie off too and set it down neatly on top of his coat, so no part of it touched the dirty ground. He left his T-shirt on.

Sid began shuffling light-footed toward him. He used the ties on the train track to measure his footwork. He'd push off with his back leg, launching himself forward one tie-length, and then another. He came in quick like that, forcing Jamie backwards.

Sid hadn't even thrown hands yet and Jamie was already struggling, finding it difficult to keep his footing while moving back.

"Pay attention," Sid said, and swam forward, swinging those long, looping hooks and haymakers he liked. Jamie sprang back to get out of range, but he caught his heel on one of the ties and fell on his ass on the tracks. Sid showed no sign of giving him space and kept coming, so Jamie placed a hand on the cold steel of the rail, got his legs underneath him, and jumped forward at his brother, glancing his fist off the bony ribs that stretched down from Sid's collarbones like the railway track they stood on.

As payment, Jamie ate a couple shots underneath his armpit and a half-power shot to the ear, which filled it with the rushing of high tide and the red-hot throbbing of blood. Sid choked his next breath in and slid a few steps back, still smiling, and took another pull from the flask while Jamie righted himself, grimacing.

They'd learned a little boxing because their father had taught them, Sid mostly, when they were little, when they'd just visited, before their mom died and they got stuck with him all the time and it stopped feeling like an adventure. And word had got back to Jamie that Sid had been spending some afternoons with one of the old guys at the church, who also taught boxing here and there. And Sid had been bringing back old videotapes—Jamie didn't know where from—of the early UFCs that he plugged into a VCR—which he also didn't know where it was from.

"Come on," Sid said again, and they met again, and separated, and again, and spun, two partners in a dance. It was mostly Sid as the aggressor, with Jamie on the defensive, trying to keep outside his brother's range, and covering up against Sid's favourite trio of half-punches when he couldn't. The constant retreat wore on him as it always did eventually, and Sid appeared to forget the feeling of Jamie's knuckles against his ribs and swarmed forward without hesitation, giving Jamie no time to collect himself. His shoulders tensed and bunched up around his jaw, and Sid pressed on, touching him almost at will—not too hard, but never ending. His brother's hands grazed his arms, pecked at his temples, kissed his nose.

Jamie wasn't trying to win. He didn't even want to win—that would have meant really landing on Sid and taking the small moment of joy his brother found in victory away from him. Jamie was trying to lose, which in a way turned it into a win. It would help Sid, somehow. Or he felt like it would. But his fist twinged, cried out to be thrown. That's why he'd grown reluctant to fight with Sid—not because he hated it, but because he didn't. He wanted to lash out too, but he knew he just needed to eat these shots. Just take them. He needed to be the charcoal, just for now. But Sid was landing on him, over and over, fists like whips, and Jamie began to lose track of them, lose his ability to anticipate them, lose his footing, lose control.

He retreated straight back along the tracks, and straight back again, and again, and Sid chased and chased, then Jamie retreated a half-step only, dug the balls of his feet into the rocks, twitched his hips, and fired his right hand down the middle.

He felt Sid's cheekbone through the light pillowing of skin that covered it, felt it roll and bounce across the ridges of his knuckles as his fist scraped off his brother's face. Sid's head snapped back, and he fell. Jamie rushed toward him, reached out for him, to hold him, help him up, but he froze and just stood over him, shaking his tingling hand. Sid crawled up to sitting, bent forward over the tracks, legs splayed to the sides, and cradled his face in his hands, the hunch of his back and shoulders rising and falling with each deep breath. Finally, he looked up and smiled. Sometimes hitting him earned his wrath, other times his respect. "Where did that come from?"

Sid laughed a rusty laugh and rubbed his cheek. It glowed rose. Jamie reached down to touch it, but Sid flinched. He stopped laughing and made no effort to stand, just looked past his brother down the tracks to the corner the train had come around seemingly only one time before. He put his hand to the rail. He put it back to his cheek.

Jamie offered him a hand up and left it hanging in space until his brother finally accepted it. Sid lurched to his feet, meeting him chest to chest when he rose, his exhale sour against Jamie's face. Sid turned, following the tracks back toward town, curving his steps in the long, slow arcs of the quietly drunk, bouncing back and forth between the rails.

Jamie ran to catch up, also unsteady, legs still shaking.

"Sid," he called. "Wait up."

Sid did not wait up, but Jamie caught up with him easy.

"Where you going?"

When they were off the tracks, and down the road, and up into the field where the wind always seemed to be buffeting the long grass, Sid finally said, "Dad should have fucking been there with him, at the end."

Jamie should have just taken the beating from Sid, let him get it out. He shouldn't have fought back, not really.

Sid clenched his fists at his side, his hands white and his knuckles brushed a soft red from earlier.

He should have just taken it.

Sid spat angrily, and the wind caught it and dragged it back along his cheek. He wiped it away with his fist.

"So what are you gonna do? Try to beat him up?" Jamie asked. He reached out and grabbed his brother by the shoulder.

Sid spun and slapped his hand away. "Why not?" His jaw was clenched, and each breath pushed spit out from in between his teeth.

Jamie should have been charcoal.

"I won't go with you," Jamie said.

"Then don't."

"I mean I won't come back. At all. Not if there's two of you."

Sid spun, fist cocked. It shook. "Why don't you hate him?"

"I do, but... I think this is what he wants. I won't give it to him."

"I have to," Sid said, almost pleading with him.

"You don't."

"Well, I've got to do *something*." He rubbed his fist against his eyes and turned slowly home.

Jamie watched his brother's bony back until he disappeared and then he turned his gaze around the field, watching the land stretch out away from him.

# Chapter 5

**HE'D SORT OF PROPPED HIMSELF** up on his bed so he could look down out of the window. He'd been doing it a lot in the mornings, afternoons. The neighbours' cat was fat and patrolled around their backyard and then leapt, in two tries, onto the fence beside his house. The fence was thick—their dad had liked to build sturdy; he hated sobering up to do things so much that the idea of doing them *again* was unacceptable—and had a four-by-four post running along the top, which meant that the cat, inelegant as it was, was able to plod down it and lie in a loaf near the centre of it. A bee buzzed somewhere near the cat's head, and it swung a slow paw and missed and almost unbalanced itself.

"You used to be a hunter," Jamie said. Did he know the cat, from before? How long did cats live? He drove the dull tip of his index finger into the glass a couple times. "Hey, cat," he shouted. The cat lobbed itself into the neighbours' yard and scrambled into their house. And then Jamie was just staring through his window at the fence. He hoped Sid hadn't heard him shouting to the cat, if he was even home.

When he was in the gym, he was always up before dawn. Even when he started making a bit of money and rented a house for himself and some of the guys on the team to live in, he was in the gym first thing every day. He wondered if he'd never be able to break that habit. And he feared what it would mean for him if he ever did. But he didn't have anything to get up for, so he just stared out the window, remembering. There was nothing to see, just their little backyard, and then some other empty, greying yards, and then the ridge, which was empty as far as he could see it from there. He did that until something forced him to get up for the day.

"Come on," Sid said. Jamie hadn't heard his brother coming. He just appeared in the doorway. This was only the second time Sid had come to wake him.

"You want to go to the cemetery again?"

Sid made a fist and pressed it against the door frame. "Just come downstairs," he said, and then he disappeared.

Jamie shrugged down the stairs a minute or so later, dressed and trying to shake some life into his limbs.

Sid waited in the kitchen. "Don't think I've forgotten, little brother." He pulled a half-burned cigarette from the ashtray, took a long drag of it, and flicked it out the window. The butt thunked off the edge of the window frame, leaving a small smear of ash. There were two plates with chocolate muffins on them. Sid slid one across the counter—the sound a distant grinding of stone over stone. A little pink candle pierced the top, the flame leaning and flickering weakly as it moved.

"Got it from Mack's Market down the road. Remember Mack's? Still there. Don't worry, I paid for it this time." He laughed. "Go on."

"What's this?"

"It's a fucking candle and a cake, man. Well not a *cake* cake. But you know. For your birthday. You've been gone a long time, yeah, but not so long I'd forget that. Thirty-one years old."

It didn't *feel* like his birthday, but the little candle burned beneath him and flickered in his breath and told him that it was. He knew what day his birthday was, he just hadn't realized that this was that day. Living here, away from everything he'd grown to know, left him feeling like he was drifting, outside of time. His schedule had been the gym's schedule. They kept track of things for him. And in general he'd started to have a hard time remembering dates and things over the last few years, so he'd leaned on them even harder for that and they'd been fine to do it. No one to do that for him since he'd left, and no reason to either. And what was a birthday actually measuring if he couldn't fight anymore? Another year of what? He was thirty-one now. Would thirty-two look any different at all? Thirty-three?

He sighed, the slow blast of air battering the little candle and knocking the flame out cold. He blew harder on its smoking corpse, in the hopes that Sid would think it had been on purpose.

"What did you wish for?"

"Not supposed to tell, right?" Jamie said, shaking his head and trying to drive out the feeling of sliding his gloves on.

They pulled the muffins apart with their hands, ate them standing up in the kitchen.

"Dex used to love these things," Jamie said. "Remember?"

"Yeah. They'd make him crazy. Send him through the roof."

Jamie held a piece of the muffin up to the light. It was so sticky with sugar and fat, it barely crumbled.

"God, I bet he'd be great, you know? A great guy."

"What?" Sid asked, looking genuinely surprised. "What are you talking about?"

"I guess I just think...he was always the best, you know? Really nice. I think if he'd have made it, then... I don't know. I don't know how to say it. But don't you think of it? What it would be like if he was still around?"

"No."

"Just no?"

"No, I'm glad. He got out of here. He got *you* out of here. That's something. Best case. If nothing would have happened to him then you would have stayed here too and you both would have... turned out like—"

"No way. He was different. He would have been different."

"There's no different out here. We're all just out here waiting and when you can't wait anymore you do something you don't want to. That's all there is. He wasn't different, he was just younger."

They finished the rest of their muffins in silence and when they were done and wiped their sticky fingers mostly clean on the fronts of their jeans, Jamie picked up the candle, pink with white swirls, and spun it slowly between his fingers. There wasn't a package for it on the counter like the muffins.

"What's this?"

"Candle?" Sid said, and twirled his finger around his temple.

"No, I mean like, why do you have pretty pink candles?"

"Been in the drawer for years. Got 'em for my daughter. Didn't know if they'd still light. Do candles go bad?"

Jamie felt like he had to sit down, but there was nothing in the kitchen to sit down on. He grabbed the edge of the counter to steady himself. "You've got a daughter?"

Sid grabbed the plastic wrapping the muffins came in and the paper baking cups with the crumbs stuck to the sides and threw them in the trash. And then he plucked the pink candle from between Jamie's fingers and threw that in after.

"Yeah. You're an uncle. But I don't see her much anymore. Not since Dad died." Sid dropped his arm onto the counter and swept the plates he'd set their muffins on into the sink, where they landed with a crash.

"Why, what happened?" Jamie asked.

"Happy birthday, bro," Sid said, and he sniffed and reached toward the ass end of a bottle of Worthy's from the counter, but Jamie shot his hand out to it first. Too early for that kind of thing. But he wondered what Sid would do in this first time Jamie'd ever tried to take control of anything since he'd been back. Sid was teary-eyed and he retreated to the doorway, waiting to be asked something, maybe, or waiting to be told something. But Jamie didn't know what to say and just patted the shoulder of the bottle and nodded to him, and Sid turned and walked up the stairs.

Sid had a daughter, and Jamie hadn't known. In all those years—he didn't even know how many. Did she know about him? But why would she? He was not there, and if something hadn't gone terribly wrong for him, he never would have been. What else didn't he know? When he'd thought about this place, he'd thought about it as the type of place that never changes. And in some ways he'd been right. It was the same as it had been, just a hell of a lot closer to death. But in other ways, obviously, that was untrue. There was some life here still, hanging on somehow against day after day of empty tides.

One of the plates in the sink was broken. Jamie picked the broken bits out and piled them in his hand, and when he'd got them all, he angled his hand over the trash, the sharp white shards sliding down off his hand, piling up like the fragments of bone he'd watched them dig out of his hand during his first surgery.

**THEY PIPED IN MUSIC THROUGH** hollow, rusty-sounding speakers in the evening. Old rock and pop from the sixties and seventies mostly. And it was a little darker, the dirty yellow bulbs strung along the ceiling giving less light than the window did when it was daytime. Those were really the only ways the Anchor was different in the evening. Same assholes at the bar, same woman behind it.

He got there a little before seven and she offered him a coffee or a soft drink. He declined. "I'll get milk in for next time," she said. She winked at him, and then led him into a small closet off the back of the bar, where there were a couple boxes of bottles on the floor, some shelves with bar supplies, a sticky stereo system with wires that led right into a hole drilled through the plywood wall, and a small assortment of old clothes and dusty mementos shoved into the closet corners that had pictures pinned to them.

"You work every day?" he asked, before she could start.

"I have a woman I bring on here and there in the summer or if I need a few days off for whatever, but otherwise it's not busy enough to justify hiring someone. I don't open early, and I don't stay open late, so I'm okay."

"Oh, this is your place? Like, you own it?"

"Of course. Do you know many bartenders that can just decide to hire on a whim?"

He flushed. "I don't know. I guess I just thought . . ."

"Can't own a bar because I'm a woman?"

"No. What's that got to do with it? No, because you're so young."

"I'm a year older than you, Jim."

"You look younger," he said, but that wasn't why he hadn't thought she could have been the owner. It was because he thought they were about the same age, and he was nowhere near being able to own a business. The distance between what he knew and what somebody would need to know to run a business was . . . a lot more than a year's worth of work. He wouldn't even know how to start.

"Well, you don't look too youthful, so I don't know what kind of compliment that is." She slapped him on the shoulder. "I've already given you the job, Jim. No need for the flattery."

"No one's called me Jim since school," he said. He still couldn't remember her name, and it was too late to ask. In the gym when he'd forget people or things, which he was starting to do a bit—things had been getting cloudy—he could just ask someone else to remind him. It didn't matter. It was almost expected. But he was the new blood here. He'd never felt less like the big dog than he did now. "Do they... what do they call you now? The same, or...?"

She squinted at him. Being a big guy made it hard for him to shrink, but he wanted to. She was on to him. "You can't remember my name!" She put her hand over her mouth. The one piece of jewellery she wore, a thin silver bracelet, hung slack as her jaw.

He put an arm out and leaned against one of the plywood shelves. It creaked under his weight, and the music cut out.

Her eyes were not shut, but drawn close and shining, wet at the edges. Her teeth white and bared, mouth wide. She was bent forward at the waist, one hand clawing into her own stomach, her other reaching forward and steadying herself against his chest while she rocked with laughter. He flexed under her touch, set himself to studying the photos in that little closet. Many were her. She had different hair. He could feel the gears turning, but they were turning slow. He knew he knew her, but the details were stubborn coming.

"I know who you are. I do. We went to school. I just, I'm not good with names anymore. Can't keep them in my head if I'm not always using them."

She righted herself and dabbed at the corner of her eyes with her wrist. She shook her head. "Wow. Well, see if you can puzzle it out, *Jim*. This is too fun to just give up."

She went back to orienting him about the work, her spiel interrupted occasionally by short bursts of laughter that she worked quickly to get back under control. He missed a lot of what she said, too embarrassed to think of anything else.

He sat in the same stool he had when he'd come in those first days, though he pulled it apart from the rest, put himself right beside the door, and sat with his arms crossed, intending to check the IDs of everyone who looked like they needed it.

That ended up being nobody. He eyed anyone who seemed like they might be getting a little bit loud and stole looks at the bartender when he thought she wasn't paying attention to try and jog his memory. He had a memory, sudden but hazy, of kissing her. But was that actually a memory, or just what he was thinking about?

Occasionally he got up and did a stroll through the room to collect any empty glasses left on those small tables against the wall, so she didn't have to come out from behind the bar. He'd put the glasses on the edge of the bar and watch her while she worked. And she'd catch him looking and he'd pretend he'd only been waiting to catch her attention and roughly shove the glasses toward her with his meaty fist, nearly toppling them or sending them off the back of the bar. Then he'd nod and return to the stool and do the same thing an hour later. The only thing that changed was how drunk the others got. He remembered the sound of her laughter echoing off concrete.

In between all that he'd try not to think about how a couple years before he'd been paid two grand to spend a day at the opening of a supplements store.

She did last call at eleven, and most left grumbling within a half hour. After that point it was just Paul, stubbornly holding on to the last few sips of beer, and Colin, who seemed only to be waiting for Paul.

"Time to go, Paul," she said. She always seemed to use his name.

"*He* gets to stay," he said, jerking his thumb toward Jamie.

"Well, he's helping out here now, and you're not."

Paul raised the glass to his mouth and kissed the liquid inside, but Jamie didn't think he drank anything at all. He made no effort to move. Colin reached over and grabbed his arm, but Paul jerked away from him.

"Time to go," she said again.

He didn't respond.

Jamie eased off the stool and walked up behind the two old men. "She said it's time to go. So, it's time to go."

Then Paul slid the bulk of him off the stool and turned around, getting as close to Jamie without touching him as his belly would allow.

"Is that so, *Champ*? And what are you going to do if I don't? Ultimate fight me?" He laughed. It was an awful sound.

Colin got up from the bar and pulled at Paul's elbow again.

Paul took his hat off, dragged a hand through his matted, receding hair. He smelled of beer and sweat and musty clothes. He squared up on Jamie, cocking his hands up in a fighting stance—hands too low, elbows flared—with his cap squeezed out awkwardly from one of his fists. Still laughing. Braying. He jerked his hands in slow, lazy impressions of punches. Empty promises. "Think you could beat me up with your karate?" He dropped his hands to his sides. "So what would you do, huh? If I didn't want to go."

She moved to come out from behind the bar, but Jamie waved her off.

He took a step to the side, so there was nothing in between Paul and the door, and swept his hand out in a graceful arc, gesturing to it. "I'd do whatever I wanted. Good night, gentlemen."

Colin grabbed Paul's arm, saying, "Sorry. Bye. Bye. So sorry. Bye."

Paul allowed himself to be dragged out, occasional chuckles still coming like a car sputtering before it died. He resumed his shit-talking by the time the door shut behind him, telling Colin all about what could have happened in there if he hadn't have wanted to be the bigger man. Jamie made sure the door was locked and then returned to her. She was leaning across the bar, face arranged in half-mock surprise.

"What was with him trying to fight you?"

Jamie slid into a seat, still warm from someone else.

"People always try to pick fights with me, to prove themselves, you know? Always some loser out there trying to become a winner off you."

"That ever work for them?"

He shrugged. "Anybody can land a lucky punch... but it would have to be *real* lucky. Real lucky. I don't know anybody that lucky. What's that thing you said last time about paying for everybody?"

"Ah. Fishing's dried up for him, same as everyone, but before that happened, he did better than most. His dad was a real man, I guess, and Paul inherited a decent collection of ships. He couldn't lose money faster than his dad had arranged for him to earn it, so he has a lot more than most of the guys in here. It's nothing you can count the days by, but it's not unusual that he covers the whole bar when they all settle up for the night."

"Huh."

"Yeah."

"Paul?"

"Yeah."

"Huh," he said. "Can I get a beer?" He tapped his fist on the bar twice and let his breath out. Paul, a success. Wasn't that a fucking thing?

She poured him one and slid it to him and he sipped it and let the chill of it soak through the glass into the heat of his hand. He didn't like the taste too much, but he liked the understated coolness of it.

"Why d'you think he does that, then?" Jamie asked. "He's some kind of secret nice guy then?"

"I don't know."

"Real well-kept secret, if he is."

"I haven't been able to figure it out, honestly. Sometimes I think so. Other times I think he's just buying the company.

Other times I think he loves people owing him. And other times I don't know if it even matters."

"How could it not?"

"All the same to the other guys, isn't it? Their glasses are full. Anyway, enough of him. You got rid of him for the night, so let's be rid of him."

He nodded.

"So you remember me yet?"

"It's not that I didn't remember you, just that... anyway, yeah," he laughed. "Erin. Erin... Uh, I still can't remember your last name. Sorry. I have a hard time keeping track of things sometimes." He'd only remembered about an hour before, but now that he did remember, she flickered with familiarity, with certain expressions or movements he'd seen before—or, rough drafts of them.

She thought a moment, rolled her eyes exaggeratedly. "You know, there was a time I worried I broke your little heart, but I see now that's not the case. You've forgotten all about me."

He squinted at her.

"We kissed once," she said. "Remember?"

Few things from his past here that didn't involve Dex or fists stuck out as anything but vague impressions. Nothing he remembered felt as exciting as kissing a girl. He wanted to remember, though. He tried hard to remember. And when that failed, he tried to imagine it. She looked strong. Wouldn't turn to nothing in his arms. But he wasn't great at imagining, either. "Yes," he lied. "I remember. I kissed you. Out by the..."

She pretended to look shocked. "*I* kissed *you*. Once and only once. But then my dad said if I got mixed up with a Stuart, he wouldn't get me a car once I could drive. You seemed nice enough, but that was an easy decision at the time. Blame your dad for being such an asshole. He might have cost you getting laid."

"I'll put that on his tab. Your hair's different."

"I used to straighten it in school so I'd fit in. But do you know how long that shit takes? I gave up on that not long after I graduated. And anyway, the type of guy that comes into this place is gonna hit on me no matter what my hair looks like."

"Why wouldn't they?" he said, and then quickly dropped his gaze. He shouldn't have said that.

She grabbed her bar towel and threw it at him in one quick motion, a snap of the elbow and a flick of the wrist.

He slipped his head off centre and the towel hit the wall behind him with a damp smack.

"Impressive," she said.

"You learn to avoid things flying at your head when those things are hands and feet."

"Well, you'll have my hands and feet to worry about if you don't get back to work."

It didn't take them long to close. The place was small, she was practiced, and he was quick. They didn't talk much. After his initial burst of excitement, he grew quiet again, didn't know how to talk anymore. It had been easy, and then it wasn't. He was realizing just how many of his conversations with the guys had been all about training or eating, and how little his thoughts on the best protein-heavy snacks would mean here.

She dropped a zippered bag full of cash into a lockbox fastened to a shelf under the bar, and she handed him some cash, two crumpled twenties.

He looked at it under the light.

"What's wrong," she said. "Expected more?"

"No... why?"

"You look like you did when I left you at the quarry, like, fifteen years ago."

"No, this is fine," he said, and shoved the money in his pocket. "Thanks."

"Now don't say anything else about it or I won't invite you up for a nightcap."

She flicked the switch in that little closet, dropping them both into the darkness of the room, him blind but for the ghost of a light that slipped in through the window—like when he used to walk through the gym down before dawn, feeling nervously around outlines—and her striding so quickly and confidently through the dark that it may as well have been light.

**HER MATTRESS WAS ODD, OR** he felt odd on it. It was big enough for him to stretch out on. It wasn't a couch at a friend's or a single held over from his childhood. He didn't wake up curled into a ball or with limbs hanging down to the floor. He just rolled over.

Erin was already awake. She had good shoulders, good definition in them. Maybe from lugging boxes and barrels around. She looked concerned.

"You've got some explaining to do," she said.

He jolted up right, the sheet coming free when he did. He covered himself with his hands. "Why? What?"

"You were... I don't know how to describe it. Sleep fighting?"

She laughed when she said it, but it was fractured, a bit more nervous than her easy laugh the night before. His laugh, by comparison, was easier. He'd woken himself up doing that before, kicked his blankets right off him or punched his bedside table. When he laughed, she relaxed. She got up to make coffee, still naked, padding from her bedroom out into the hall. She had great definition on her calves. He hadn't noticed that before. He heard a grinder.

Her apartment was above the bar. The building was old and a little worse for wear, but it was clean. Almost the opposite of Sid's house. Which was actually his house, though he didn't think about it that way. Hung from the wall opposite her bed was an old fishing net, thick rope with crap hanging off it, driftwood and baubles and whatever.

She came back in with two cups of actual, real coffee, and sat at the foot of the bed and looked at him expectantly.

"What's that?" he asked, gesturing to the net.

"It's, uh, art? I don't know exactly. Why, you want to buy it?"

He quietly took a sip of his coffee.

She laughed again. She did that easily. "Don't worry. No one does. But I still make them. Got a box full of beach finds in the closet."

"Why do you make them if nobody wants them?"

"Got to do something in my life that doesn't revolve around the bar," she said. "Anyway, do I have a bruise?" She pulled at the skin under her eye, stretching it exaggeratedly wide. "I think you caught me once, with your thrashing." She pried her eye open as wide as it would go, covered it with a cupped palm like an eye patch. Eventually she took her hand away from her face. "Apparently humour is not an essential skill for cage fighters."

"Martial artist. Cage fighter is... I don't know. It sounds bad. Makes me sound like a thug. And the cage is actually for safety, not for... whatever other reasons you'd think. Stops you from falling out when you're grappling." He tried to move into a grappler's pose, but he was still holding the coffee and a bit spilled on his bare leg, and he stood up and used the still somewhat swollen blade of his right hand to brush it off. It didn't hurt as much as he'd expected—the burn or the hand. He was still naked. He sat back down again, tried to cover himself again.

"Okay, mister martial artist. Why the sleep fighting?"

"It's nothing."

"It doesn't seem like nothing."

"It's just dreams."

"It doesn't seem like it's *just* dreams."

Jamie scrunched his face up and looked out the window at some seagulls circling above the harbour.

"Well come on then. Spit it out."

He sighed. "Okay. Fine. Remember when I first came in here and I talked about that guy Tamura? That fight I lost? I dream about him. Every night almost."

"Dreaming about men, huh?" she said, and she laughed.

It was a happy, birdsong sound, but her comment had shut him down and he couldn't take any joy from it. He looked down at his cup and ran his finger round the edge of it.

She lay back across the end of the bed, feet dangling off the edge, resting the coffee on her stomach. "So tell me about it. And you should take this as a compliment, because dreams are fucking boring, and I never want to hear about them."

"I just dream the fight, over and over. Sometimes he finishes me. Very rarely I finish him. But mostly it's just as it happened."

"And how's that then? That it happened."

He shook his head. "Nah, you don't want to hear it," he said, while he put his cup down on the bedside table and sat himself up so he could gesture more clearly. "Well, he was an Olympian, right? They thought he was going to be a big star. Well, he is, so they were right. But they thought he was better than he was back then. Thought he'd throw me on my ass and that would be that. But he was too green, and too small for the division—the Japanese don't cut much weight, so they're often undersized when they fight westerners."

"Isn't that unfair?"

"No one makes 'em not do it; they just choose not to." He shrugged. "It's a bit of a trade, strength for speed and endurance. Anyway, he was short, and he was still green with his striking, and that meant he couldn't close the distance to grapple me without getting hit in the face for the effort."

"And what exactly do you mean when you say *grapple* in this context?"

He lunged forward off the wall and dropped himself on top of her, chest to chest. She exhaled a bit, her warm breath tickling his knotted ear. Her coffee spilled a little on the blankets beside them, but she didn't react to it.

"I mean this," he said. "Got you down now. Could do whatever I wanted."

"And what is it that you want?" she said slowly. She raised her one arm up and grabbed him firmly behind the shoulder.

He pulled away from her, righted himself, oblivious. "Every time he got close to me, I'd put my jab into his face, and if he tried to push through that, I'd pop him with my right. Wobbled him a couple times that first round. He was breathing hard and spitting blood halfway through. I was getting close to finishing him and he knew it. So near the end of the round he came in and I hit him with my jab and he just closed his eyes and drove toward me with everything he got, so I loaded up my right hand and fired it with everything I got."

He mimed the combo, made a popping sound with his lips when he reached his full extension.

"And what happened?"

"He was lower when he came in than I expected. I don't know if he tripped or just adjusted his game plan, but his head was lower, and I almost put my fist right through his frontal lobe. Broke my hand a dozen places. Couldn't feel my arm. I dropped him, but the round ended before the ref got close enough to call it off, and he got up and wobbled over to his corner, and when the next round started he had mostly recovered and I could barely feel my arm. And we both knew I couldn't throw that hard again, so he chased me around and pressured me into the cage for the next two rounds and that was that. Majority decision Tamura."

"And that's what you dream?"

"That's what I dream."

"Not a happier ending?" she asked.

"Not usually. It's not really a dream," he said. He put his now empty cup down on the bedside table and propped a pillow up behind his neck. The spines of some of the feathers pushed through the pillowcase and scraped his skin. "Like, it comes in my sleep. But, it's more like a memory. No, more like time travel. I just go back there every time I close my eyes."

"What's Sid think of all of that?"

"I don't know. Nothing. We don't really talk much. Well, we talk a lot, I guess, just we don't say much."

"Why not?"

"I don't know. Just, it's hard. We've got no...habit of it. So there's so much time to cover. And also, I don't see him much. He works or sleeps most days, and then he's out most nights with friends I guess."

She barked with laughter. Loud and involuntary, but quickly brought under control.

"What?" he asked.

She shook her head, and he sat up and lowered his voice and repeated himself.

She sighed, put her coffee on the floor, crawled over beside him. "Sid's not out with friends. Sid's dealing. That's part of why he's barred everywhere."

"Sid doesn't sell drugs," he said. "Fucking...drugs." He was so frustrated at the idea he couldn't even articulate it. Once he'd fought someone he knew took 'roids and was so mad about it he refused to knock him out in the first when he could have. Instead, he let him hang in there and punished him for fifteen whole minutes until he couldn't stand when the decision was announced. That was one of the things he was most ashamed of, but the idea that someone would want to fight with an unreasonable strength advantage made him instantly furious. "Just, he doesn't sell drugs," he said.

"Okay," she said. She put an arm around him. Her hand clasped his far shoulder and it was hot from where it had held the mug. Her arm across his back felt heavy and cold. "Should we get going now?"

It was an awkward way for her to change the subject, but he was grateful for it. He didn't know how to end the previous conversation, and he definitely didn't know how to keep it going. He rolled himself out of bed and shortly they left her apartment above the bar and walked up the switchback hill to the hospital, which for some reason embarrassed him to even be near, recalling his previous mix-up with the doctor. He prayed Erin wouldn't ask him what was wrong, but she didn't even seem to be paying attention to him. She was staring out over the ocean, taking big deep breaths though her nose like a yoga person.

They walked down the hill to the beach in The Shade and then began to cross the narrow scrub of anemic sand—a small sliver between the murky ocean and the bank of weeds that sloped up to the nearest housing development—but it was rife with piles of washed-up detritus from the ocean. Once, when he was a kid, a severed foot had washed up from the sea, still in its sneaker, though Jamie hadn't seen it. Sid said he'd seen it, but he'd been lying. For weeks after, boys would throw sneakers at each other, and especially at the girls, announcing they'd found another washed-up foot. He wondered if anyone had ever explained what had happened. If they had, no one had told him.

As he and Erin walked together they scanned for unusual shells or driftwood to decorate the fishing nets she hung up. Their looking down while they walked caused their paths along the beach to hourglass them toward and then away from each other. Erin picked up sea glass and an unusual twist of plastic, and she put it all into the bag that hung from the crook of her elbow. She talked to Jamie about her dad, how he hadn't been able to handle it here as what often felt like the only non-white person in town, and left soon after Jamie had. Jamie had never seen her dad, hadn't known he wasn't white. He realized that meant she also was not white, though he never guessed it. He wanted to ask her a whole lot of questions then, to just sit down and have the types of long conversations people did in movies, but didn't know how to start, and he didn't know what *not* to say if he didn't want to say the wrong thing, so instead he bent down a picked something up that she might like.

"Do you want this?" he asked.

"A yogurt container?"

"No," he said, looking closely at it, and then he dropped it.

"You're just going to leave that here?"

"No," he said and he bent back down, even though it tweaked his back a bit, and put it in his pocket. That seemed to move the conversation on from the things he didn't know how to ask about. But nothing replaced it, so they walked in silence, until he saw something else, a shell like in that famous painting of the naked lady coming out of the water. It had a pearly pink sheen and was shaped like a fan, and it had both halves still stuck together—hinged at the base.

"Hey, what do you think of this?" he said.

"Oh, wow," she said, when he handed it to her. "Clam shell, but you don't normally see them intact like this. Thanks, hunk," she said, and she kissed him on the cheek and she didn't hold his hand, but she did put her empty hand briefly on his back and steer him straight so they walked along beside one another. And then her nose began to twitch in this very cute way, and he was going to say something about it, and then she said, "Ugh, do you smell that?" And before he could respond she sniffed at the clam shell and recoiled, then tossed it spinning behind them.

"Sorry," she said. "Nice find, but it stinks."

"Couldn't you clean it or something?"

"I could, but I'd have to break it open and I've already got lots of halves of those. I was excited because it seemed like something new."

He turned and looked at the shell in the sand behind them, somehow not wanting to leave it behind, and then in the following silence thought of what she said earlier about Sid, not sure if he was mad at her for saying it, or mad at Sid, or himself.

A FEW EVENINGS LATER, JAMIE was sitting on his bed, again staring out his window in the early evening, wondering if he should go down to the Anchor or if that would be weird. Did their sleeping together mean they were dating? Was it a mistake that had already or would someday cost him the job? He didn't know. People invariably got into relationships with each other at the gym. There were about four times as many men as women, but when a woman joined up single or became single while training there, she usually ended up dating one of the many waiting guys. But they didn't officially work for each other. And even so, when it eventually went south, almost always someone ended up leaving the gym. It was too hard to train right when people stopped talking, the silence too imposing, too big a barrier to work around. He'd avoided ever getting into that kind of mess himself, but strangely he felt himself almost mirroring the experience of that disruptive silence here with Sid.

The last time they talked was when he'd asked about Sid's daughter—god, he didn't even know her name—and Sid had walked off, and Jamie'd just let him. Jamie'd spent a bunch of time at the Anchor since then, and he knew Sid slept and kept odd hours, but he still felt like he hadn't really seen his brother for a conspicuous amount of time. Every time the conversation got difficult or uncomfortable, which was often,

Sid got quiet, or had to go, or just said he had to, and then Jamie wouldn't see him for days, after which Sid would act like nothing had ever happened.

The door closed downstairs. His brother was home.

"Oh shit," Sid said when Jamie came downstairs. "You didn't run off again after all." He looked drunk. "Thought you might have moved out already." Sid grinned. His lips raised sharply at the edges, like a cursive V, like the Grinch in the old Christmas cartoon they watched when they were still with their mom. It looked like a smile, but it didn't feel like one. "I brought food," he said, and he hefted a couple of white plastic bags bulging with steaming Styrofoam cartons.

"Everything okay?" Jamie asked.

"What do you mean?"

"Nothing," Jamie said.

Sid poured himself a generous drink and they ate standing up in the kitchen. There was a small selection of limp salad tucked in by an afterthought, but otherwise it was all unhealthy. It all had been lately. He'd always eaten healthy with his fighting friends, or, during lean times, he hadn't eaten at all. But since he'd come back, almost every meal had been bad. Sid had bought them cheap burgers from that last remaining takeout joint, which was attached to the gas station. Fatty meat with fatty sauces, and fries and onion rings. Fat and carbs and fat and carbs, with a tiny bit of protein for colour. He felt tired all the time since he'd been eating this way. But he did eat it, because he was hungry and couldn't afford anything else, and because he didn't know how to tell Sid he didn't want it without hurting his feelings. And also because he was starting to want it, starting to realize that the moments where he shovelled that garbage down his stupid mouth were some of the only good moments he had in any one day.

"What do you think would have happened that day if I didn't hit you?" Jamie asked.

"What are you talking about?" Sid asked through a mouthful of fries. "When did you hit me?" He pressed his fingers against his jaw and cheekbone confusedly.

"When we were kids. The day I left. We were on the tracks and I cracked you and you got up all pissed and went after Dad."

Sid looked away a long time, finished chewing, took a long drink. "Never thought about it."

That was a lie. It had to be. Jamie had thought about it every single day since for over fifteen years.

"Probably the same thing," Sid said, and he shrugged, and he went back to eating, and Jamie ate too because he didn't know what else to say.

After, Sid got a couple crowbars and a handsaw from the shed, and then they moved the furniture away from both sides of the first wall they were going to bring down, the one where Jamie had driven the hammer through a stud. It had hung there for a week like a light switch in the off position, waiting for someone to flip it and get this whole job started again.

"Well, we can saw a shallow grid into the wall and pry off the sheet with the crowbars, we hammer through in between the studs, or . . ."

"Or?"

"You could . . ." Sid dropped the tools on the floor, held his arms above his head, and screamed, "Hi-ya!" as he did his best *Karate Kid* crane kick. He landed off balance and stumbled into the side of the bookshelf. A loose photo which had been leaning up against the dusty books on the shelf fell over.

"I don't think I want to do *that* exactly," Jamie said.

Sid straightened himself up. "No, not exactly like that." He stepped away from where he had been standing, as if distancing himself from the action itself. "But you know. Something. Show me something."

"I don't know. Maybe we should just use the tools. Like, do it proper."

Sid smiled. "You'd really get to fuck this place up."

Jamie pulled the sledgehammer from the wall and tossed it over onto the couch. "How far apart are they? The wood beams. Studs are they called?"

"Sixteen inches or forty centimetres, whichever works for you. And there might be wire running across the bottom, I can't remember, so give yourself a knee-high grace unless you want to knock the lights out."

"You're asking me to risk kicking through live wires, and it's the lights you're worried about?"

Sid waved the concern away. "Bah. You'll be fine. You're a big guy. Not enough in the house to hurt you."

Jamie made a fist and set his left hand under the hole he'd already broken, and then slid it to the side, the paint rubbing against his knuckles, scratching an itch. He fired a left hook through the painted drywall, and it came out the other side. He made a note not to hit so hard, advancing across the room delivering a series of left hooks that punctuated the studs. And then he threw a couple front kicks, driving through to his knee. And a jab and a left uppercut. And a left and right up-elbow.

It wasn't long before he leaned over and put his hand to an as-yet un-assaulted section of the wall and leaned against it, pressing his forehead against the surface. He used to go for hours. And the wall wasn't even hitting him back. He'd punched and kicked at the wall until the fatty monstrosity his brother had brought him for dinner threatened to come back up, and now he was hunched over and heaving breath. He felt a light slick of sweat at his hairline, and the wall now had a couple dozen holes of varying size smashed through it, but it was standing just fine. He hadn't, as he'd hoped, brought it down around him with his fury. He'd barely scratched it, really.

"That's pretty much it," he said, "what I can do here. A lot of the rest... even sixteen inches or whatever, I might clip myself on."

"Cool," Sid said—a bit flatly, Jamie thought. He didn't know what else he could have done. What else did Sid expect of him? Some Thai people could kick down trees. Jamie had never been that good at it, even when he was good at it. But still, he'd like to see Sid try. Show him how easy it was.

"Great job," his brother added.

Sid cut a grid into the wall, and they each took a crowbar and leveraged out the drywall, Sid using both hands and Jamie just his one. The broken stud and all the holes seemed to be making things harder, but there wasn't much to do for it now. Sid kept offering Jamie a drink as they worked, and Jamie kept saying no. And Sid left his own empty at his feet, seeming to hang his permission on whether Jamie would join him.

After they'd taken one full side of drywall and plaster down, they moved around to repeat the process in the other room, and Jamie asked, "So what exactly do you do, again?"

Sid looked over at Jamie's section of the wall. "Exactly what you're doing is fine. You're going fine. A little slow, but..." he teased.

"No, I mean, exactly what do *you* do again, the ninety percent of the week you're not in."

"This mostly," Sid said, without taking his eyes off the work.

"Just this?"

"This, that, whatever. Beggars can't be choosers, you know? And there's not a lot of money for something like repairs or renovations in this part of the country anymore, so I got to just do what there is to be done. Just got to take what comes."

"Ah."

"Why?"

"No reason."

"No. Why?" Sid stopped what he was doing. He was on a small step ladder, prying the wall from near the roof. He looked down at Jamie, the angle even steeper this way than it had been when they were kids. "Why?"

"Nothing. Just, Erin...nothing. Hey, you ever heard of James Braddock?"

"Why, is he bothering you?" Sid said, raising his arms again to the ceiling.

"No, he's dead."

Sid froze, turned to him wide eyed.

"From old age. I think. Not from me."

"Oh, okay. Fuck." He laughed, shaking up on the little ladder, and Jamie started to step forward, to reach out for him, but Sid steadied himself and said, "I was almost really impressed by you."

"He was a fighter, during the Depression. He broke his hand and went on welfare."

"Great fucking hero to have."

They pulled more sections from the wall, dropped them into piles, each new addition a dusty slap.

"He picked up work on the docks when he could, but he had to use his left hand for everything, because his right was in a cast, see? So he does this a while and when he eventually gets his comeback shot, he goes on to do even better than before. Wins a world championship even."

"No shit?"

"No shit. Because he had a lot more control over his left hand now, a lot more strength too."

Sid crossed his arms. His hands were caked with white dust. He left palm prints on himself. "That's cool."

"Fucking right, it's cool. It was a hell of a story. Legendary. They called him the Cinderella Man."

Sid clapped, and the dust burst from his hands, and he laughed and inhaled it and started coughing in a fit cured only by a long drink of whisky, the tumbler wrapped by a series of dusty, white handprints like it had been analyzed at a crime scene.

"Look at you plotting your fucking comeback as the fucking fairy man. Jesus. You had me going, you fucker. Fuck me," he said, and he reached for his empty glass again. "You want another drink?"

"I'm good, thanks."

"Alright, Cinderella, suit yourself. But I'm getting one." He strolled into the kitchen to refill his drink.

Jamie walked back over to the bookshelf and lifted the loose photo that had fallen over on the shelf. His dad's face looked back at him. He was younger then. Younger even than Jamie was now maybe. His face was big, took up the left third of the photo. It looked like he was smiling. The rest of the family was close behind him. All of them. His dad squinted in the photo, seemed unsure of the camera.

From the floor near the sofa, Sid's phone beeped.

If it had been Jamie that lived in this house when their dad had died, he would have bagged up every picture, every personal belonging, everything he'd even showed the slightest affection for and thrown it out with the trash. Wouldn't even have given it the importance of burning it. Just dumped it in the street. There were other photos in the house he would have put out—ones of just them, just the brothers, just their mom. There had to be.

Sid returned with his new drink.

"Why've you got this here?" Jamie asked.

"Just never got around to getting a frame for it. I can get one for it, if you want." Sid's phone beeped again, and he picked it up and read the message. "Shit, sorry. Got to run. You can finish that now you've started, eh?" he said and gestured to the battered wall. "If not, don't worry." He threw his drink back in one and walked to the door.

"No, I meant like, why've you got a photo of him? Why's he here at all?"

"Well *he* was here," Sid said, and slammed the door behind him with a force that spun the drywall dust all up in the air.

Jamie waited long enough to be sure his brother wouldn't burst back through the door having forgotten something, then he walked to the kitchen where the bottle of Worthy's sat on the counter, and Jamie faced off against it for so long the lights seemed to shift behind it, and he poured himself one and then another and then walked back out of the kitchen as the house creaked and groaned around him, settling in with its new damage, and he walked up the stairs, past Sid's room, past his, to their dad's.

When he'd first got back, he'd assumed their dad's room was the same as they'd left it, since Sid hadn't moved into it and Jamie's room and the rest of the house were still the same. But Sid had told Jamie he had a daughter, and he realized that he'd seen some of their dad's things in the shed when he'd gone in after the bag.

The shape of the room was the same—bed in the same place, wardrobe in the same place, desk and chair in the same place. But the bed was a single with curling, white head and foot boards and pink blankets with cartoon characters he didn't recognize on them. The wardrobe was new and short and white, didn't lean to the side like it was going to collapse. This desk had a mirror attached. The chair was a rocker piled high with cushions.

When Jamie had opened the door to his room a few weeks before, it had been musty even though Sid seemed to have been expecting him and had opened the window. This room wasn't musty. There was the soft whir of a dehumidifier in the corner, and there was a plant on the windowsill that looked real, and alive.

He felt like he was trespassing, disturbing someone even though there wasn't anyone there.

He closed the door and went back downstairs. He got another drink and then another and then pried the rest of the sections of wall off and collected them together, but he was clueless about what to do about the two by fours still stretching from floor to ceiling and fastened tight, so he left them where they were, standing between the two rooms like prison bars.

## Age Twenty-Two

It was loud in the city in the morning. Loud and dark. The sounds of the people outside and the traffic, even early, came in through thin windows and rattled around against bare brick walls and woke him most days well before he'd have liked.

He stayed in the room filled with bunk beds above the gym—which he guessed was as close as he'd ever get to living in a university dorm—for visiting fighters, other people who wanted to do camps without the distractions of home, and in his case, the people who didn't have one. Sometimes it was busy and had a warm energy to it, but now it was only him. He was the only full-timer there. Except for Robbie, obviously, but Robbie had his own little room on the main floor near the boiler.

Robbie had retired after an eight-fight losing skid. When he was fighting, his nickname had been Hands of Stone, but all the punishment he'd taken in the ring had made him slow and now some of the younger guys called him Head of Stone behind his back. He lived in the gym because even before that last skid he'd never really made it off the regional circuit, so he didn't really have any money.

Jamie crawled out of bed and grabbed the pair of shorts he'd hung from the window to air out. He didn't want Robbie to hear him. Robbie had trouble sleeping and always came to work or talk with Jamie when he heard him up, but he was too much. He tried too hard.

The sun wasn't there yet, but it was coming. All the sky he could see through the window was pale, steel blue. The stairs down to the training area creaked. He walked down carefully, pausing every time they cried out and waiting until the silence resettled, reminding himself he was allowed to be there.

He chose not to flick the lights on. He'd just work with the growing dawn that fell in from the high windows. The bag his dad had made at home, the handmade, keg-shaped, brown leather one that sat mostly untouched in their shed, hung down to Jamie's waist and was for punching only—"manly" in the traditional sense, but restrictive.

They had that kind here too, but his choice was new and black, from Thailand, narrow around—he could wrap almost all the way around it with just one arm—but long, the bottom swinging only inches above the polished concrete floor. There were other types as well—teardrop-shaped ones, inverted teardrops, and an array of Tetris shapes fixed to the walls—but he liked this one, how it was somewhat familiar in shape but new in purpose.

He circled slowly, just touching it, just working through the movements he'd been refining since he'd arrived. He extended a jab, just until it met with resistance, and then twisted his hips and slowly extended his right cross, until it too just barely touched the bag, as if to wipe a tear from a cheek. He had an urge, whenever he threw that right, to drive his fist right through the leather. To punish it. To pack everything that had ever happened into a single shot. But Mo had told him that this was not the point at all. Not of training, and not of martial arts. It's not about negativity. It's not about destruction. It's just the opposite.

So he circled around it, barely touching it, moving through the motions slow and purposeful like dance steps. Jab, cross. Jab, cross, hook. Jab, cross, hook, uppercut. Jab, right low-kick. Left hook, right low-kick. Over and over. Slow and steady, until as the light rose and the bags became clearer in their definitions, stopped haunting the edge of his sight.

He'd come to like this time of day almost immediately, even though he still felt a touch of uneasiness. Even when there were other people in the dorm, the first hour or two of light downstairs was almost always his alone. He'd never had time like that before, that was just his.

"Hey, boy," a voice called.

Jamie threw his arms up in a motion halfway between defence and surrender.

He heard Mo laugh. "Easy, boy. Only me." He waved his hands and sprang effortlessly toward him like a gazelle. Mo was shorter than Jamie and had a considerable wrapping of fat around his whole body, even on his shiny, hairless head. But he was powerful, and moved quickly and gracefully, and Jamie, though much leaner and younger, struggled to match his speed.

"I don't know how you do it. Floor so cold this early," Mo said, still bouncing from one foot to another. He'd closed the distance between the two of them almost instantly.

"It's the type of thing you can get used to," Jamie said. "At least it's dry."

Mo looked curiously to the roof. Looking for leaks maybe. "Well, not me," Mo said, and he led into the same bag Jamie had been using. Opened up a few slow punches and kicks—spine straight, Thai style—and finishing with a series of explosive right hooks that bent the heavy bag in half. "Hap," he shouted with each impact. "Hap, hap, hap!" and his shouting and the leather bursts of his punches was the end of the peacefulness of Jamie's morning. Mo leaned around the bag and smiled. With his pudgy face and medium-brown skin, he looked a bit like the Buddha, but missing his two front teeth.

"Come on," he said, "onto the mat."

When Mo's feet touched the thick foam mats of the training area he sighed, like he'd just lowered himself into a hot bath, and shook himself, noodle armed, from the shoulders. He put his hands up. Jamie did the same. He could see him now, at least his outline, his edges, defined and growing clearer. Mo moved toward him. Jamie backed up instantly. It was one of the few things he hadn't had to be taught. He maintained distance automatically. Mo pawed a few slow hooks through the air. Jamie raised his left hand up to just above his ear and took the first shot on the arm. They weren't wearing gloves, but they weren't even really making fists.

"Got a call last night," Mo said.

Jamie froze. Mo's hand, arcing through the air at the end of another right hook, swung in and landed clean on the side of Jamie's head. Mo tapped him on the cheek with his fingers. "Wake up, you."

"Who from?"

Mo, his hand still against Jamie's head, messed up his hair and laughed.

"Adam," Mo said, and Jamie laughed now, too. "You know him, Adam. From King's. Has an amateur kid wants a bout."

Jamie slipped a jab that never came and came back with a right. Mo didn't move or parry, so Jamie tapped his fist on the man's smooth chin. "Hap," he whispered. He tried to start them moving again. He shuffled back and forth. He circled to Mo's left.

Mo just stood, heavy and still. "Serious," he said.

"I don't know, Mo."

"What's not to know?"

"I don't know."

Mo's eyes flashed down to Jamie's feet. "What are you doing?"

"What?"

"Moving, look." He pointed. "You're backing up, like I'm trying to fight you. I'm not. I brought you something. A gift. Good news, kid." He threw his arms up in the air. "What, you want to just stay here forever and play on the mats?"

Jamie shrugged.

"Come on," Mo said. He shook his head and took Jamie by the arm.

Jamie stumbled a step, trying to keep up.

They sat down against the cool gym wall, knees tucked up under their chins.

"What's the problem?"

By Jamie's foot, one of the puzzle tabs that locked the mats together was bent somehow upwards, and he worried at it with his toe, trying to smooth it out. The foam was smooth, but not too smooth, and soft, but not too soft, and had no discernible texture. It was most easily identifiable by what it wasn't—the cold, hard concrete floor beneath.

Mo sat quiet while he finished and tucked it down nice and neat.

"You don't want to get hurt?"

"Nah, that's not it."

"Then what? Don't want to hurt anybody?" He snaked a quick hand out and slapped Jamie on the top of the head in the same place he'd mussed his hair not long ago. "What's hurt? That's hurt. Slap. Hurt. But now it's not. Hurt goes away. It's nothing. And the boy wants a fight? Doesn't care about hurt, or he wouldn't ask. Injury, now that's something... But you're not going to injure anybody." He laughed, and his face looked round and smooth and innocent like a baby's. "I've been hit by you!" he shouted. "You're not injuring anyone!" He slapped Jamie on the shoulder, and Jamie had to brace against the mat to save from being pushed over. And he laughed too, a bit. Mo calmed himself down. "I joke. I'm joking. You're powerful," he said. He flexed his bicep and winked. He pushed him again. "But you'll be fine. Promise."

Jamie fussed with the mat, even though it was fine.

"Hey," snapped Mo. "Cut the shit, boy. You're needed. Yeah, *needed*. That kid out there. He needs someone. He can't fight himself." Mo jumped up and spun. He swung punches through the air at his own head, did his best to slip out of their path. The light came in bright now from the windows up high, falling on Mo almost like a spotlight. He threw an uppercut to his face with one hand, brought his other across to defend. He kicked himself, awkwardly bashing one leg against the other, eventually catching himself behind the knee and tumbling to the floor, laughing the whole time.

"You see?" he said. "Silly. Don't do that to him. That kid, he doesn't know you, but he needs you. So you'll help him, yeah? We all will. Daddy Mo with his fists, bang bang, and Uncle Paolo with his pyjamas, woo woo, and little Jamie. Safe. All of us. Together. And Robbie, too, I guess." He nodded and fired two punches into the air. "Bang bang. So what do I tell him, old Adam? That I got a man here in this family who'll step up to help a brother?"

"Yeah," Jamie said, and his breath shuddered. "Yes," he said again, so quickly he surprised himself. "You've got someone like that. I'm it. I'm in." He smiled. They smiled at each other. It was going to be good. He'd never thought about it too hard before, but this suddenly felt like exactly who he wanted to be.

Mo laughed and threw phantom punches, pumping his fists back and forth like pistons so quick Jamie couldn't even really see them, he only felt them as gentle promises on his stomach, ribs, and finally his chin.

"Okay. I'll call him. I'll tell him. Now get cleaning. People showing up soon."

Then Mo skipped, childlike, across to the office, and Jamie heard the front door cry out as someone opened it, and his skin prickled in the cold that comes from letting the world in.

# Chapter 6

**AT FIRST IT LOOKED LIKE** a scar, but in some ways, it was the opposite of that. A scar signified improvement. A surgery made you better, supposedly. Or at least it represented an attempt—effort, activity. At first it looked like a scar, but it was the opposite. He was getting worse, not better. There was no effort, no action. It was a seam of raised flesh—no, fat—that stood in between his abdominal muscles, a mountain range that separated one side of his stomach from the other, that separated the present from the past, rendered it unreachable. He'd seen it first when he was sitting up in bed and wondered if he'd still been halfway in one of those dreams in which he lived in the hospital because his body was betraying him.

After he showered, he stood naked in front of the mirror long after the steam escaped through the small bathroom window and the cold air had pimpled his skin. The ridge was still there on his stomach, and he noticed that the flesh on his waist and hips pushed tighter against his underwear than it used to, out over top a bit, too. His cheeks were fatter, rounder than he remembered, the line of his jaw less sharp. The more he looked in the mirror, the less he recognized.

Every fighter ballooned up temporarily after a fight, after starving themselves for weeks or months to make weight and then finally being free to eat again. But this wasn't that.

Nothing about this felt temporary or reactive. It had settled into him, or he into it.

He held his hands up, squeezed them into fists. They felt weaker. But his right hand didn't hurt, not unless he pushed it. And the swelling had gone down, the colour faded almost to normal. Everything else was getting worse, but his hand at least seemed like it was getting better. If it would, if it would really get better, he might be able to fight his way out of this shithole after all.

He wrapped himself tight in a towel, even though he was alone in the house, and walked to the stairs, occasionally pressing a hand, hesitantly, against his belly, his hips, his face, trying to map for himself this new and unforgiving landscape.

There was a letter for him on the floor under the mail slot. Handwritten. An actual letter, not a bill or formal notice of a contract being terminated or otherwise not renewed. He opened it right there in the hall. The writing was awkward, even by his standards. The letters themselves almost looked like they'd been written independently of each other and then just assembled on the paper, and there was a noticeable downward slope to the lines as they moved across the page.

He knew it was from Robbie just from the state of it.

*Dear champ Jamie*

*How are you? I don't know if you'll get this but I got your address from the internet. I remembered you telling me once the name of the town you come from and there's only one stuart living there. I tried to call you some times. I don't know if you got them.*

*Are you coming home? I talked to Mo about walling my room in the Gym in half so there's a place for you when you want to com home. I live back at the Gym now, we gave up the house after you left because we couldn't afford it without you, but it was great while we had it. This is great now too. Being back at the Gym.*

*I've got a lot of ideas. Now you're not so busy like before I want to tell them to you.*

It went on for four pages. He didn't read the rest. Every word, no matter how inane, reminded him of fighting, of the gym, of what was now off-limits to him. He couldn't bear it. He was almost getting by without that being his life, but only because it was entirely separate from him. He shoved the letter back into the envelope and opened the front door. Their garbage can lid was held open by scraps of sheet rock and bits of wood that were too broken up for Sid to want to keep. He tossed the letter in with the rest of the things that were now too damaged to be of any use or value.

ON THE WHARF WHERE JAMIE sat a moment before work was a solitary man who walked around to run his eyes over the boats and make sure they were all fine. Jamie watched him for a while before he went in. The old man walked back and forth along every branch of the dock, always going the exact same speed. Never slowing, never hurrying. He reminded Jamie of one of the monks he'd seen on a trip to some kind of monastery—his head was still ringing from the loss and Robbie had been pretty useless for reminding him where they were going, and why, and with who—only this man would stop every once in a while to pull something from his coat pocket and bring it to his mouth or, occasionally, toss it to one of the many screaming gulls that followed him patiently back and forth across the boards.

In the Anchor there was a guy sitting at a table against a wall who Jamie hadn't seen before. There were lots of people like that, lately actually. And definitely a few more people in there than usual. Erin had admitted to him one night across the pillow that as much as she thought she could use an extra hand sometimes from someone she didn't think would keep asking for more work she didn't have, and as much as she thought it would be nice to have an excuse to spend time with him again, she had also hoped that his being there would be something of a novelty in a town where nothing was ever new. Seemed like maybe it was working a bit, though he hadn't been there long enough to know for sure. Maybe this guy was one of those guys, who'd come in just for Jamie.

He watched the guy sipping his beer and listening to the conversation at the bar. The guy caught him looking a few times, just like Erin had on the first night when he'd been trying to steal looks at her to figure out who she was.

Some people said of boxing that it's all about lying. Lying to your opponent—convincing him you're going low when you're really going high, convincing him the shot he just landed didn't hurt as much as it did. And lying to yourself—that you're unbeatable, that you won't get hurt, that you'll be alright in the end.

Mixed martial arts didn't work that way. It was going up against an opponent who knew exactly what you were going to do and doing it anyway. It was seeing every possible way you could lose, and still finding a way to win. Until you didn't. Everyone loses eventually. You just always think it will be later.

So, Jamie hadn't ever needed to be good at subtlety. He was good at knocking holes right through the middle of things. That approach wasn't working for him now, when all he wanted to see was if he knew that guy or when he was going to finish his drink.

The guy caught him looking again. "I'm not fucking doing anything," he said.

Jamie held his hands up in surrender.

The guy got up and muttered, "Jesus fucking Christ," as he walked past Jamie and out the door, glass still a quarter full on the table.

Jamie wondered if Dex would have turned out to be good at talking to people. He had been as a kid. But maybe he'd have become quiet, like Jamie and Sid had. Would they even be friends, if his brother had lived?

Jamie collected the glass and gave the table a quick wipe with his hand. Erin pulled the last bottle of Stella from the fridge. He brought her a box from the back.

"You're really *on top* of things today," she said, ripping the box open. He blushed, returned to the door. He hadn't come back since he'd left on Sunday morning. He had wanted to but hadn't known if he should. He was used to his social schedule being determined entirely by his training schedule. He didn't really know how to measure it right when he wasn't restricted like that. He'd been embarrassed when he walked in, not knowing how she'd react. And she'd laughed at him about something in his first minute through the door in a way that told him she didn't feel weird. But he still did a bit.

ONE GUY JAMIE HADN'T SEEN before seemed to hesitate when he was leaving, as if he was going to try to square up, but he didn't. And Paul left without issue when they closed, and Jamie took a seat at the bar while she did the cash. She poured herself a beer and him a glass of the milk she'd gotten in for him.

"You were really dialled in tonight," she said.

"It all came back to me."

"Keep it up and I might slide an extra five into your pocket at the end of the night."

"Just five?"

"I'll slide it *deep* into your pocket."

He laughed, and she kept at her cash.

"What's the next thing for me to learn?" he said.

"About what?"

"Work. What's the next thing to learn to do?"

She pushed the cash away, pulled her beer closer. "You're doing great, but that's it. I worked here a couple days a week and did the books for the old owner, and then I sold all my shit to buy it off him when he'd fucked it up so badly he was willing to wash his hands of it. Now I do all the shifts and the books on top. I do fine, but it's not like I'm set to expand. So if you're looking for, what's it called, upward mobility, you're shit out of luck, I'm afraid. There's just what you're doing."

He finished his milk.

"Get you another?"

"Could I get a beer?"

"Hey, party animal, look who's coming alive after midnight."

She poured him a beer and herself another too. He made a face when he took a sip, and she laughed at him.

"I mean, you can buy it from me, if you want," she said. "For the right price. The bar, I mean, not the beer. That's on me."

"I've heard I might have a brand-new fiver headed my way, if that's the right price."

"She's a small business, but she's not *that* small."

He got up and started pulling the chains of the neon signs in the window, flicking the bar sign by sign further into the darkness, taking his time between them. "Honestly I have no idea what I'd do with a bar, and I couldn't afford it even if I did."

"Couldn't you?" she asked. She'd gone back to the cash and was dropping coins one by one back into the plastic cash tray.

"Nah, I'm broke. Well, not quite broke. I've got like, a hundred? A couple hundred maybe? I don't know. My very last ever last sponsorship cheque came through a while ago now, and it wasn't a big one."

She finished her cash and put it in the lockbox, then set about wiping down the bar, but she was moving slowly and missing spots. When she wet her cloth, she wet one for him too, and threw it across the bar to him. She missed him by a good arm's length, but he pulled it out of the air without a problem.

"Shit, I thought you just worked here to pass the time. How the hell are you broke? You're like, an international athlete, right?"

"Well, I was only just breaking into that higher tier with my last fight, and I haven't earned much since. A bit training, but that... and then, like, living's expensive in the city. I'd rented a house for me and the younger guys, and stuff. The up and comers. They paid what they could, but it wasn't a lot."

"Well, how much were you making then?"

"Hard to say."

"How is it *hard to say*?"

He slumped behind one of the little tables, threw his rag down on it.

"Well, like, I can tell you how much I was contracted for. My last fight was for sixty thousand."

"Huh," she said. She nodded slowly to herself. "That's a lot."

"I would have gotten another sixty to win, and my next three fights on that contract would increase by ten each side. Before that I signed for a flat fifteen a fight as well as sponsorships and seminars, but I don't know how much of that I actually got. I've got to pay my management fee, training fees, taxes, rent, probably some other stuff. I don't really know. I just trained and fought. Mo dealt with all that stuff for me. I don't know numbers or anything. Didn't exactly shine in school, as you know."

"Mo?"

"Manager."

"How do you know he didn't screw you over?"

"What?" he said, almost shouting. "Mo? Nah. Why would he screw me over? Nah. He's like my... well, he's my manager. We're a team. He's a good guy."

She finished cleaning the bar and came out and started on the tables he'd given up on.

"But like, how do you *know*? I couldn't even understand how old Jack used to get me to do the books here. I could have told him anything and he wouldn't have known better."

"I didn't have time for that kind of thing. I just trained. On the road by dawn, in the gym in the morning, home again in the afternoon for food and shower and a nap, and then back in the gym for the later afternoon and evening to repeat. Home to shower and eat and go to bed. No time in there to learn accounting. And if I made the time for it—well, my opponent wouldn't. I'd have my nose in a tax book or whatever and he'd be in the gym working to kick my ass. And anyway I didn't need to know because Mo knew for me, and, like, if he'd been screwing people, then someone would have said something."

"Who'd have said?"

"I don't know. Someone. I don't know. I wasn't getting scammed. I just didn't save anything. I was only just starting to earn real money. And I hadn't saved. You don't think of it, of the future. I was twenty-eight when I fought last. Twenty-eight. I've got so much left. I can lift a car, push a car up the hill to the hospital—at a run. I could kick through an oak door. Kick down a tree maybe. Why'm I thinking about saving for retirement? That's for old men."

"Because you can get hurt, obviously."

"Well, yeah, I can see that now, but you can't think like that. Can't let it in your head. You've got to be invincible, in your head. Otherwise you can't go in there at all. Then you don't make anything." He threw his rag over onto the bar. He hadn't thought much about this before. Just taken it as the way things go. But now his face was starting to glow embarrassed like those last neon signs in the window. They'd gone to the same shit school, so why did she know all this and he didn't?

He'd thought his earlier success had meant he was smarter than people thought, but maybe it meant the exact opposite. "Listen, I don't really want to talk about this anymore."

"No problem," she said. She finished up and hung the rags to dry and flicked the last of the lights off. From somewhere in the dark, she said, "There's a lot for us to do that doesn't involve much talking at all."

**SHE'D KICKED OFF THE COVERS** some time in her sleep. He woke when it was still dark. When she woke up, not long after him, she rolled over to face him. They could see each other in the moonlight that reflected in off the harbour. "You're staring at me," she said. "That's weird. And you're still wearing this." She reached out and tugged on his T-shirt. "That's fucking weird too. Not off to a great start this morning, Jim. Let's hope you get your shit together a bit by the time I'm back with coffee."

The T-shirt was one from his gym. It said NorthStar Fight Club on it and had a silhouette of a guy throwing a knee. All his T-shirts were from the gym or his old sponsors. He hadn't bought anything but jeans in so long he wasn't even sure he knew how to shop. Everything else he got given as a part of some deal.

She came back with coffee.

"Trade you this," she said, raising one white mug, "for that," and gestured to his shirt.

"I'll bring you one. I've got plenty."

"That one, now."

He shook his head. She put the coffees down and reached out, curled her fingers in the hem at the bottom and started to drag it up.

"No," he said, maybe a little bit louder than he'd expected, and held it firmly down over the seam of fat on his stomach.

She wrinkled her nose at him and grabbed her coffee and they took the same positions they had the other mornings, her stretched across the foot of the bed with some of the duvet balled up beneath her head and shoulders, him sitting up with his back against the wall.

"Even if you make your comeback like you think, you'll eventually have to retire anyway. And you won't be satisfied with the lifetime of weekend bar help, so what then?"

"I don't know."

"Yes, you do. I can see it in your face."

He took a drink, then pressed the cup against his lips.

"Get that out of the way, or I'll choke you with your fucking T-shirt."

He put the cup down on the bedside table.

"When we were kids," he said, "our dad—"

At the mention of Jamie's dad, she pretended to spit, and he got in a good laugh before going on.

"He'd take us down to a beach. An empty one. You know what the beach here is like, so he'd walk us like, thirty minutes down the coast. And then he'd beat the shit out of us. It was to teach us wrestling, he said. And we did learn to wrestle. But it was really just an excuse for him to beat the shit out of us, when he was sober enough to feel like he needed an excuse. That's what I want to do."

She sat up, leaned away from him such a small amount someone else might not have noticed, but he always did. He couldn't not see it now. "You want to beat the shit out of kids?" she asked.

"No, fuck," Jamie said. "I'm not a...I'm not...fuck it." He got up and started pulling his jeans on. "I'm remembering some things now I'm back here. Remembering about what it was like here."

"I'm sure, Jim. I was kidding. What is it that you want to do?"

He continued dressing, but less hurried than before. "I just want to like, I don't know, teach kids to wrestle or something.

Not like my dad, but do it for real. Like, for kids who don't have anyone else to show them."

"That's great. I think it's a great idea. I don't know if this is useful, but the Health and Welfare office, or the Employability and Welfare office, or whatever it's called now, is still open down in Prince William. Maybe they'd know about some funding to get a program off the ground for someone who's under-employed, like yourself? But really, I think it's great, honestly. What's Sid think about it?"

"Haven't told him."

"Why not?"

"I don't know. We don't talk about things like that. We just sort of talk shit."

"Well, I think it's sweet," she said. She reached out for him, but he waved her hand away, waved the whole idea away.

"No, it's not *sweet*. It's just…whatever. It's stupid."

"It's not stupid. I just didn't expect it. Didn't know you had any experience with kids."

He'd reached the stairs that led to the front door of her apartment. She lived above the bar, but the entrance was on the street. He only just realized how white everything was. White walls, ceilings, furnishings, appliances. Light carpet. It was all pretty new.

"Well, I've got other experience," he said, and he pulled on his trainers and sunk down the stairs.

"You don't have to go, you know. I'll stop asking stuff like that if you want. But I'd like to hear more about it. And I don't know, maybe I could help you look for funding or something for it. Like a real proper program. If you want. But we don't have to."

"No, it's not that. I've just…got a lot on today. Busy day. I'll see ya." He cast one glance back up the stairs to where she leaned against the wall, side lit, staring down at him, unmoving. She'd felt bad a minute ago for upsetting him. He'd heard it in her voice. But now she looked annoyed at his leaving. He didn't want to go. He wanted to stay with her. But their last conversation before bed had been one that made him look like an idiot and this one had too and he just needed to be somewhere now where that wouldn't happen again. He needed to go home. Sid wasn't smarter than him and even if he was, he kept it to himself.

Jamie closed the door gently behind him then hunched his shoulders up around his ears and walked away from Erin's. The roads were startling in their silence, though they were not much quieter in the small hours of the morning than they were at the height of the day. The ocean made the same noise and there were not many people that walked around in the day anymore. It's just that the ones that were out were *always* out. And Jamie wondered now if the people who lived here— *really* lived here, unlike Jamie—didn't groan and grumble, cough and scuff their way unnecessarily loudly through the streets when they were out, almost as a way to broadcast to who or whatever might be listening that they were still here.

Jamie realized he wasn't heading home and then he realized that must be because he had no faith Sid would be in, and he didn't want to confront that empty house. And then when he started taking shorter steps and longer breaths he realized he was walking up the hill to the hospital. He couldn't tell why he would do that. The sun wasn't even fully up yet, just now reaching those first few fingers of thin light from the horizon, the town not yet awake. At some point halfway up he saw a bench by the sidewalk looking over the town, and he groaned when he sat on it. There was an inscription that said "For Nancy, who loved this brightest view in her darkest times." He didn't know of Nancy. He had never noticed the bench either. The inscription said it had gone up two years after he left town. But he appreciated it. He rubbed his stiff knee absently and looked over the top of the town to the hillside opposite.

Security floodlights shone on an abandoned building site on the otherwise empty hillside. He'd heard about this from Sid and some of the idiots in the bar. Apparently the idea was to build holiday homes for people that wanted to get out of the city, but didn't want to live in any of the shitty houses the locals had been trying to sell for years. So a developer from out of town brought in a construction crew from out of town to build ugly houses for people from out of town. Except that there was no airport nearby, no train station. The drive was long and tedious and the one road up from the city flooded several times a year anyway. And then if anyone did manage to get up here, what would those rich fucks have found? The world's shittiest beach and a lot of bitter people. So they didn't get any down payments on any of the houses and they ceased construction, and now they paid a couple guys minimum wage to look over the site until they could find a few free minutes between profitable projects to tear it all down and fuck off back to where they came from.

While he waited for the stress in his lungs, the pain in his knee, and the apprehension about returning to that empty house to all reduce, he looked across at the shadowy skeleton of the old new development, where the lights that shone were cleaner and brighter than anything in the town.

**ONCE HE'D GOTTEN USED TO** waking up in the gym every morning to the noise of the city, to the squeaking, rattling chains of the wind-chime heavy bags that always seemed to be gently swaying when he wasn't looking directly at them, he'd start the day by throwing on his shoes and sweats and a hoodie and heading out into the street.

He used to run five miles every morning. That wasn't the workout. It was the wakeup. The work came after—the morning of strength and conditioning with ropes or tractor tires or the prowler sled, and after the extra-long lunch, an afternoon with the other full-time guys, and then after a nap, an evening of skills on the pads or the mats. About twelve hours every day, off and on. The running was just to get his blood moving. It barely even sweat him.

Today, it was fucking killing him. His legs were so heavy. He hadn't gone a mile by the time he first had to stop, bent double at the waist, heaving breaths, trying not to vomit.

He used to run off blindly to some unknown avenue and feel his way back later. It was how he finally got used to the city, by letting it take him where it wanted to that day. He couldn't make that work here. One way led to a narrow, hungry, dead end at the mouth of the sea and the others had landmines—winding and twisted streets and paths out a way from town that led to the cemetery, or circled back to the hospital, or went to the old train bridge, any one of which would take his legs out from under him as he passed, and he didn't have the unconscious familiarity any more to avoid those places without thinking about them the whole time. It was hard to run if you had to think about it.

And when he used to run, he used to run toward his opponent. He always saw his opponent ahead of him. He'd chase them on the street so he could catch them in the cage. If he was struggling, they'd turn around and run backwards, smiling and laughing, the shame he felt at his weakness would keep his feet moving. He didn't have an opponent anymore. There was no face to put on what he was fighting against, nothing to drive him forward, nothing to run toward, nothing out there with him at all but his weight.

He'd gone barely a mile the first time he stopped to breathe. He hadn't gone two when he stopped and leaned against a low stone wall that had come up beside the road and sat breathing and wiping the sweat from his eyes, searching through the sting of salt for the faces that would drive him on.

## Age Twenty-Five

He sat backwards in the folding chair, its bars pressing cold against the inside of his thighs. His forearms rested on the top rail. This is how they put the gloves on. It was not usually how they took them off. Most times they tore the gloves off in the ring or cage after the fight, and then shoved a pair of those L-shaped scissors in between the tape and the skin of his wrist and cut him free of the tape as quick as they could. But that hadn't been the case the last few fights, and not this one neither.

"Bad this time?" Mo asked.

"Not great."

He held his breath as Mo unfastened the Velcro straps on the gloves and then tugged them off over the mass of tape-covered cotton wrapping that was supposed to have protected his hands. Mo was trying to be delicate with his fingers, but eventually he had to press his knee into the chair back to get him the leverage he needed.

Jamie whimpered as it came free and looked away ashamed.

When Jamie, Mo, and Robbie had first got into their private dressing room, he hadn't been able to wipe the smile off his face. He was a big deal. A contender. He was important. No more cramming in with everyone else on the card that no one cared about. But now he felt alone, away from the normal after-fight chatter, that brief period of community that reminded them all that opponents, potential opponents, rivals, whatever they were, they were all chasing the same dream. They were all in this together.

He didn't have any of that now. Just the cold of the chair on his skin and the sound of Mo holding his breath. But at least there was no one else around to see him like this.

"Not great?" Mo said. "What kind of answer's 'not great?' Is it bad?"

"Yeah, it's bad."

"Is it the worst?" Mo asked. He pulled the scissors out of his back pocket and rubbed them gently against the outside of Jamie's right wrist, the edges giving him an affectionate scratch, until the tip of one of the blades caught underneath the edge of the tape and Mo slowly began to chew the scissors through his wraps.

Jamie winced. "Just do it. Just get them off me. I'm not made of glass."

"Tell that to your hands, boy." But Mo did hurry, his heavy brow creasing and building rows of ridges high up his bald head. He cut the tape in as many places as possible before removing it to take as much pressure off Jamie's hand as he could when he pulled it off.

"Yeah, it's the worst."

As soon as his hand was free of the cotton and tape bindings, it began to swell.

"We'll call Doc Webb tomorrow. Get you fixed up."

The door to the dressing room swung open and Robbie burst in wearing a shiny grey dress shirt and a broad grin. Robbie had a patchy beard he'd grown when he moved into coaching—to make himself look more respectable, sage-like, Jamie figured. His eyes were sunk and often looked glassy or out of focus, like he looked at the world through a permanent teary dew. The ridges of his eyebrows, fat with scar tissue, hung heavy over his face.

He was holding a bottle of champagne in a shiny silver bucket. Instead of normal handles or rings like Jamie'd seen in nice restaurants, the handles were in the shapes of stags. Robbie carried it with his fingers laced through the antlers.

"And new!" he shouted, his voice deep and hollow, a base drum. "And new!"

"Jesus, Robbie, where'd you get that thing?" Jamie asked. *And new* did sound good but it was empty in this room and

Robbie's empty voice rattled off the walls and he already was getting a headache. Between that and this crazy bucket that now Jamie was sure he was going to end up responsible for, he really did wish Robbie would just fuck off. But he came as part of the package with Mo, so that was that settled.

Robbie looked down at the bucket. His smile faded. "Just got it from the back of some closet." He looked at Jamie and his growing, reddening hand. "How is it this time?"

"How's it look?" Mo said.

Robbie hooked his foot through the leg of a chair that was resting against the wall and kicked. The chair slid across the concrete floor and came to a stop right beside Jamie. Sometimes in all the idiocy he forgot Robbie'd been a pretty fair athlete himself.

Robbie grabbed the champagne bottle and dropped the bucket onto the chair. With his free hand he grabbed Jamie's forearm and drove his ballooning fist into the ice water.

Robbie struggled with the foil wrapping on the bottle; he had thick, slow fingers, and he was aware of being watched. When he finally got a grip on it, he pulled it off and swore and threw it on the floor, then lifted the bottle to his mouth and gripped the cork with his teeth. He pulled the cork out that way, the pop seeming to echo through his whole head.

And then he stood there, the cork clenched between his teeth like a spent cigar.

"Forgot the glasses then, Bobby?" Mo asked.

Robbie cast a searching gaze around the room. Then he held the bottle up and poured some of it into his mouth and down his chin and onto his shiny grey shirt, where it darkened a ring around his neck.

"And new!" he shouted, drops of golden liquor bursting from his mouth and sparkling in the overhead fluorescent lights like fireworks. He held the bottle out.

"I've never really drunk champagne before," Jamie said.

Robbie poured some out over the crest of Jamie's head. It was cold. And even though Jamie felt like it was a waste, the cold was oh so nice. His head was still hot, his heart still beat in his ears, his hair still dripped warm sweat onto his legs and down his back. And then the champagne, so cold, washed over him and he heard it fizz as it ran past his ears.

"Bit much, isn't it?"

"It's just what you do, boy," Mo said, "in times like this."

Robbie cried, "And the new, Kage Killers Middleweight Champion of the Wooooooooooooooooorld, Jamie—The King—Stuart!" and poured out more of the champagne, this time into Jamie's mouth.

The bubbles that erupted out of his mouth before he swallowed it rolled slow and cool down his neck and onto his chest before they all burst, and the little trickle of flat celebration rolled the rest of the way down his chest before catching on the edge of his new championship belt.

"Jesus, man. That finish?" Robbie said. "Coolest thing I ever seen. Bad ass." He shook his head and chuckled.

Robbie handed the bottle to Mo, who took a swig in the same way, lips not touching the bottle. That's how they always drank when they had no glasses. Robbie got cold sores, which were actually herpes. A lot of people had 'em, and they weren't really that big a deal, but they were contagious, and if you got an outbreak before a fight it might get cancelled on you, which would waste a lot of your time and money and make you look like an asshole to the promoter even though there's nothing you could do about it.

"Can I?" Robbie asked. He gestured at the belt.

"Yeah, of course," Jamie said, but then he inclined his head toward his hand, still in the bucket. "But you're going to have to get it off yourself."

Robbie went around behind him and peeled open the

snaps, then eased off the nearly ten-kilogram belt. As Robbie held it, Jamie got his first good look at it. It was gold plates on black leather and on the main plate were two mirrored capital Ks, and in the negative space between them was an image of a square cage, and all of that was surrounded by coils of barbed wire and then a pair of daggers.

It was big, bright, obnoxious, stupid.

"It's beautiful," Robbie said. He pulled his fingertips across the shining surface of it, and then wiped the smudge with the cuff of his shirt. He rubbed his sleeve across his nose, which was flattened and bent to one side.

"It is," Jamie said.

Mo poured himself another mouthful of champagne. He looked at Jamie and the two made a lasting eye contact. "Good work, boy." He stepped around and slapped Jamie on the back. "Good fucking work," he said, and he slapped him again, this time knocking Jamie forward in his chair. Sid had used to do that to him when they'd come back from scrapping on the tracks. He thought of his brother then, if he knew anything about what Jamie'd just achieved, if he'd care. If he was still alive.

Robbie smiled in a way that bared most of his teeth and wiped at his eyes with the cuff of his stupid, shiny shirt.

**JAMIE FIDDLED WITH THE KEY** card that unlocked his hotel room door, as his hand was currently taped into an ice-pack sandwich. When he got it, he stepped inside and turned to say goodbye. Mo pulled the key card from the door and slid it into the slot on the wall just inside and all the lights came on and they were bright, too bright, almost stabbing him in the brain, and he pulled the card out and threw it on the floor, returning himself to a comfortable darkness.

"You sure you don't want to come out for a drink, boy?"

"Yeah, Champ," Robbie added.

Jamie held his hand up. "No, thanks. Think I'm just going to take some ibuprofen and lay down. We'll go out for a couple drinks when we get home, yeah? I'm buying."

"Okay, Champ," Robbie said.

"Okay, boy. Champ," Mo said.

They both stood in the doorway though, watching him. They didn't walk away. And he didn't shut the door. They just stood there, until finally a door opened and closed down the hallway and they all seemed to snap out of it and Mo said, "Okay. Well. We'll go then. You sure you okay?"

"Yeah, Mo, just a little beat up is all."

"Not as much as the other guy," Robbie shouted, and he laughed.

"Did a damn good job tonight, boy. Did us proud." Mo held his hand out for a handshake and then looked at the state of Jamie's hand and laughed and rubbed his hands excitedly over his bald head. "Good job." He clapped Robbie on the shoulder and pushed him a little and Robbie heaved off, leaving just Mo and Jamie in the doorway.

Mo leaned into him and said, "He looked for weeks for that fucking bucket. The antlers like your crown he says. Because you're 'The King' or something. Get it? I don't know." Mo shrugged, and he squeezed Jamie on the shoulder and nodded to him and then followed Robbie off down the hall.

Jamie shut the door, and he pressed his ear to it, and he listened to them walking away. He couldn't hear what they said anymore, but he felt like he could hear the tones of their voices. Happy. Proud, even, although he thought maybe he was kidding himself on that one. But positive. And it was him who had given him that. He'd done that for them.

He slung the belt onto the bed and he lay down beside it and looked at his own reflection in it, his face taking on Picasso angles wherever it crossed new ridges on the plate. The shine on the belt was the shine in Mo's eyes, in Robbie's.

The room was dim, the light coming exclusively from one bedside lamp. It was nice. There was a double bed with a box spring underneath it, and a TV, and the carpet had been soft under his feet. And the room had almost no smell at all. It was the nicest place he'd ever been. He'd heard of all these celebrities that just live in hotels. If he ever made it off the regional circuit and into the big leagues, that's what he'd do. It would be great to have a bed with springs that still sprung, that had sheets that were clean. It would be great to be able to move whenever he wanted, to not ever have to call any one of them home.

The pat on the back he'd gotten from Mo was still echoing around inside him. He'd done it hundreds of times before but for whatever reason this time it had made him think of his brother and now he couldn't not think of him. Jamie sat up and picked up the room phone. It was white and blocky and still had the twirly cord connecting the receiver. He dialled half a phone number then hung up. He was surprised his fingers still remembered the sequence. He took a deep breath, and then another. He picked up the receiver and dialled again, this time getting all the way through the number and putting the phone to his ear, but the cold of it shocked him and broke his nerve and he hung up again. And he breathed for a bit and dialled again, and it rang, and his heart pounded in a way it never had in the ring. Someone answered.

"Hello?" The voice was quiet, but it sounded so close. It wasn't supposed to sound close. It was supposed to be far away, not there with him in the room. And it was the wrong voice.

Whatever excitement he had had in his victory, whatever joy, disappeared the instant he heard that voice again. Instead he felt that deep, yawning coldness. He pulled the whole phone out of the wall, breaking the little yellow clip. He'd say it had been an accident. He'd say he tripped. He was a fighter anyway. No one expected better of him.

He looked again at his reflection in the belt.

He stood up. And then stepped up onto the foot of the bed. And he wondered, if he hooked the belt under his chin and threw the other end around the hanging light and stepped off the end of the bed, would it fit tight enough around his neck? Would the snaps on the belt release? Would the light fixture break?

From down on the street below he heard a deep, familiar shout. "And the new, middleweight champions of the wooooooooorld, Jamie Stuart and Robbie Barrett!"

Jamie stepped down from the bed and walked to the window. Robbie was shadow boxing down the street, and just like when he'd still been fighting, he didn't seem to value head movement or defence or caution. Just charging blindly forward against ghosts.

# Chapter 7

HE HITCHED A RIDE WITH a friend of Erin's to Prince William, an hour's drive south. The friend was going to go looking through a scrapyard there. He dropped Jamie off in the town centre. Jamie was early for his appointment. He'd have liked to sit down for a coffee somewhere, or a bite, but he didn't have the money, so he walked around. Prince William was a bigger town, comfortably over ten thousand when he was a kid. Looked like less now, but not that much less. Not like home. There was still some activity in the harbour. Not a lot, but some. And there were some cars with rust spots fixed with just putty and primer, and there were some houses with broken shutters, but overall this town still seemed like it was surviving. He supposed being at the end of the highway helped. He sat in the harbour to wait. There was a group of older First Nations teens laughing and talking animatedly over milky coffee they shared from a large thermos, and some younger kids eating tiger ice cream. He was surprised by the sound of the gulls, which he hadn't realized until that moment that he barely heard at home anymore. Not like when he was a kid. Must be less to scavenge. He sat there until a church bell rang out the time, and then he headed to the office.

He hadn't washed or ironed his good shirt since he'd worn it to the hospital, but that had been a pretty short day, so it still looked okay. Good enough for this, anyway. But the shirt had come untucked a bit. He flattened his hand out like a knife and shoved his shirt back down under his waistband.

There was that swishing sound behind him of jeans rubbing together.

He pulled his hand out from under his belt. He sat up straighter.

A woman sat down opposite the desk from him. She was about his age. She had short, dark hair, wore a flowery blouse. She placed a notepad on the table in between them. She moved around in her chair a bit, unable to get comfortable, and eventually pulled a set of car keys from her back pocket and set them off to the side.

"Well, Mr. Stuart. Sorry for the wait. I mean, thanks for waiting. Trying to do that positive phrasing, they call it. You heard of that? It means less apologizing, I think, but more thanking. Apparently that's better for you. Or for me. Well, thanks for waiting. How are you doing today? Nice weather, isn't it, for this time of year? Raining, sure, but not cold. Not so cold a good coat won't do you, anyway. Have you been in before? You look familiar."

She drew in a breath. She smiled.

"I was on TV a couple times," Jamie said, slowly, "but I doubt you'd have seen it." She looked familiar too, but only in that vague way that everyone here did. Something seen and then forgotten but never really known. Maybe she'd lived near him. Probably they'd gone to the same school. But they'd probably never spoken. And he didn't want to say because he didn't want to be associated with his family and he didn't want to have to admit to anyone else that he had trouble remembering them.

"Oh, a genuine television star. Don't know as we've got much call for that at the moment, but we'll see." She smiled at him. He smiled back. It wasn't as bad there as he'd worried.

"Well, we've just got some simple questions for you before we can help you."

She had a thick fringe and her hair hung down to her jawline, curled slightly at the end. It looked ridiculous, a bit like his old boxing headgear, but he smiled.

"So, Mr. Stuart, there seems to have been some kind of error as a lot of these sections don't have anything filled out in them. Darn computers. So we'll just go through them right now. What education or qualifications do you have?"

"Never got finished school. My trainer Robbie kept telling me to finish by mail, even offered to help, but if you ever saw him trying to use his phone, you'd know how much help he would have actually been. And I just didn't know how to say that in writing. I've never filled out any applications before. Or any forms. Or anything really. My coach did all that for me."

Her pen moved quickly across her notepad as he spoke. He couldn't read it, not just because it was upside down to him but because the lines she drew came out so loose and flowy on the page they only seemed to hint at letters, but she seemed confident and never went back over her work, never scribbled anything out or rewrote it. He'd still have been scratching away at the first line.

"Sorry, who's this Robbie, Mr. Stuart?"

"Robbie Barrett. He was sort of my boss. Or sort of my employee. Sometimes, kind of my roommate. It really depended on the, uh, on what was going on at the time."

She raised an eyebrow. "Okay, sorry, what exactly was your profession?"

"When I was like, in my teens and early twenties, I worked under the table as a bouncer. But I was a fighter for about ten years, starting around the same time. That's been pretty much all the work I've ever done. I was the Kage Killers middleweight champion. And I fought in Japan. And then I helped out a bit in the gym after that, but it didn't go so great, and I mostly haven't worked in about two years."

"You were a... *cage killer*?" She wrinkled her nose as if she'd just stepped in something. "You mean like, that TV wrestling where they wear spandex?"

He sighed. "No, no. No. I'm a martial artist. *Was* a martial artist. Like boxing and judo, you know, like in the Olympics."

She perked up. "You were in the Olympics?"

He shook his head. "No, I was just... a fighter, I guess. And I was good. I was ranked. In the world. I don't know."

She resumed her place in the forms. She had cat hair on her sleeves.

"And then you were mostly unemployed for two years, you say? So how did you get by?"

"Savings."

"And how much of your savings remain?"

He raised up his empty palms. "That's why I'm here."

"Oh. Okay, then. And why did you quit, uh, cage fighting?"

"Didn't quit exactly. Just couldn't do it anymore. Got hurt." He held his hand up. It didn't look so bad. Might not even notice if you didn't know to look.

"Were you intending to apply for disability? Because that is unfortunately a different process with a different department. And between you and me, if you're walking and breathing, you've got no shot of getting on disability no matter what's wrong with you. And maybe not even then, not with this government." She leaned in closer to him, conspiratorially. "I know this man..." she started.

"No, not like that," he said. He should have let her go on, but he couldn't just accept the implication he was helpless. "I don't know much about this, but I'm not disabled like, in a wheelchair or something. I got a list of injuries, yeah, but who doesn't? I got stuff I can't do now. But I *can* do stuff. I know how to do a lot of stuff, you know? Just not like, any of this type of stuff." He waved his hand around at the desk, at her. "Forms and applications. But I'm not useless. The doc wants me to work as a janitor at the hospital. Can you believe it? A janitor. That's what she thinks of me up there. I was a world champion, you know? I'm not famous or anything, but still. I can do lots of stuff. I just can't always explain it all."

She put her pen down on the table beside her notepad. It made a clacking sound, a hard sound. "Are you saying that you have an open offer of employment?"

Jamie tucked his shirt back in.

"Because if you are attempting to apply for unemployment rather than disability and you have an open offer of employment, then I can only tell you to accept the work."

"But it's not work that... I need to do something more than that, you know?"

"And what kind of work are you interested in then? If you have experience as a doorman, perhaps we could look into getting you a security qualification."

All he really wanted was to fight again. Everything else was a compromise; it was only a matter of degrees. The physio work was one he could have lived with, the mopping up piss wasn't. Even thinking about it got his fists twitching, his shoulders begging to start rolling in their sockets.

"I don't know exactly, but like, I was a world champion. I've got to be able to do something important."

She did not pick her pen up. She didn't even move for it.

"Mr. Stuart—"

"Jamie."

"If you are not pursuing disability and do not have a plan to achieve a specific job, but you do have an open offer of employment... Mr. Stuart?"

"Jamie, please." There was gum stuck to the bottom of the desk. He kept touching it. "It's not even for me, really," he said.

"What isn't?"

"The money. I'm not like... Since I've been back here, I've been thinking of things. And now I've got sort of a plan. A project, really, that I want to do. For the community. So if I got the money to live on, I could just focus on that. Everybody wins."

"Mr. Stuart, that's not really the purpose of this program."

"Well, then what program is it? Who do I talk to?"

"Jamie... Jamie Stuart... Wait, from school?"

He snapped his attention back to the woman and her pretty shirt and the hair helmet.

"Oh my god! Jamie Stewart. It's me, Holly. Holly Warren. From school."

Holly Warren had been two years below him. They hadn't known each other, but it was a small town and he knew her family wasn't so much better than his. But here she was with her job and her fancy fucking shirts and her own desk and her car and her cat waiting for her to get home at the end of the day.

"You were just gone one day. Just gone. And now you're back." She smiled at him again, but not the same way as before. This time it was tight-lipped, narrow-eyed. She rested her cheek in her palm and sized him up like she already knew everything there was to know about him.

"Huh," she said. "Well, I'll be. People will be shocked to know you're back in town. Shocked."

"I bet."

She got serious. "Well, in the meantime, can you tell me more about this janitorial work?"

She placed the pen back against the paper and looked at him. So that was it then. Now she knew he was a Stuart there was no need to help him find anything that didn't involve swimming in piss and shit.

"I'm sorry," he said. He stood up.

"What's wrong, Mr.—Jamie?"

"I've got somewhere... I've got to go. Sorry. I shouldn't

have come here." He couldn't bring himself to turn and see how what amounted for his whole life was less than half of one page of unreadable scribbles on a government-issued notepad sitting crooked on the desk of someone who he used to go to school with, someone who thought she knew him.

**HE GOT HOME HOURS LATER** and there was an oven dish on the step with a tourtière in it, wrapped tightly with plastic, and a post-it note on top of that with his name in the doctor's handwriting. He stared at it a moment and then carried it in the house. He had no room left in his mind to think about this or what it was supposed to mean. He set it on the floor just inside and leaned against the wall.

The scream he screamed left him without him hearing it, he just felt it roughen his throat. He spun and drove his foot through the wall beside him. He didn't know if this was one of the walls that they were planning on taking down and he didn't care. He drove the point of his foot through the wall over and over until his toes caught a stud and he twisted his ankle. Then he flailed at the wall, lashing out with his fists. Not punching, just beating his fists in an impotent rage like when he'd been a child lashing out at his father, until he tired and stood heaving in the entryway, shoving tears from his face and calling himself an idiot and hammer-fisting himself in the upper thigh.

He left without going any farther into the house. It wasn't time for him to start yet, but he wanted to get to the Anchor.

For the first time in his life since his mom had died, he felt like he really needed to talk. He'd never felt like that before. Or, he'd never let himself. It was hard to tell which.

He pushed the door open almost an hour before he was due. She'd have a few minutes so he could tell her what happened, and she'd tell him what to do. She owned a business. She knew how to do life stuff.

They looked like all fishermen, same as the regulars. Stale and stout like their drinks. But the bar stools were full and the little tables across from them too, as well as most of the space in between. There were people standing in between the men sitting at the bar. He saw only the top of Erin's head, and only because he stood taller than most of the men in here, many of whom had a noticeable hunch in their backs.

He shouldered up to the bar. There were people in the way, but he moved them as easy as if they were children.

"Thank god you're here," she said.

"Something happened today."

"What?" she said. She wiped the sweat off her forehead with the back of her forearm.

"I went down to the, uh... office. The employment, uh—"

"What?" she said again. "I really can't hear you. Do you mind starting now? I can see the glasses piling up out there, but I can't get to 'em."

He threw his sweater on a box of beer in the back and picked up all the empty glasses on his way back. He looked at what was low in the fridge while she started loading up the glass washer. He brought her a few boxes of bottles and left them on the bar and posted up at the door, arms crossed, letting his eyes roam unfocused over the room.

The door swung open and Colin and Paul walked in. Paul looked at him, sizing him up almost, and then went straight to the bar, slapping people on the back.

Colin stayed back by the door. He didn't quite come up to Jamie's shoulder. He looked at him, and at the room, and he nodded.

"Don't get many good days on the water anymore. Fewer and fewer. And nothing to make up for it. So it's a big celebration for everybody when anyone pulls a good haul."

"If it's always bad now, why do people still go out?"

"What else do they know?" he asked.

"Huh," Jamie said.

At the bar, Paul tried to lean one of the other men out of his stool.

"Wouldn't figure you to be on a date with him," Jamie said.

"Ah. Not my ideal company, but I've gotten used to it. He's my cousin."

"No shit? Wouldn't have guessed." But now he looked closer, he could see a vague similarity, a sharpness of the eye that in Paul he would have called a beadiness, but just made Colin look like he was paying attention. But it was there.

"Anyhow, this seems like it's going to be too much of an evening, for me. I'm going to go and buy a couple bottles of wine and listen to the radio at home. Save Paul the expense of my tab." He placed a hand just gently at Jamie's elbow. "Good night, James."

"Night."

A few hours later when Paul emerged from the bathroom, fly down, he staggered back, past the ass-end of the pint he'd left on the bar and he walked up to Jamie.

"The champ," he shouted. "Everybody watch out!" He cycled his fist through the air like an old-timey boxer. The rest of the men at the bar turned to look, but quickly turned back to their drinks and Erin. She poked her head above the crowd, squinted at him, but her attention quickly went elsewhere.

"World champ. Big tough guy," Paul said. None of the others bothered to look over this time. "Hey?" he yelled. He shouted a laugh across the room. "Ha! Big fancy tough guy, in here with us." Still no one looked, no one laughed with him, no one cheered for him.

He turned back to Jamie, got really close. He smelled like old sweat. He fixed him with his beady eyes, breathed sour into his face. Jamie's eyes started to water. "Y'act so fucking great because you used to climb up on a stage and wrestle around with some dude in little shorts like some kinda homo, but you got a piece of shit life like everyone else and a piece of shit dad, a piece of shit broth—"

Jamie didn't let him finish. He stepped out from between Paul and the door, grabbed his arm, which was thick but offered little resistance, and jerked him forward. Paul staggered a few steps and Jamie shoved him through the door.

It wasn't a real move. It was never anything he'd learned or trained and wouldn't have worked on a professional. But he knew it would work here. Paul was old and fat and dumb and his strength, which may have been considerable once, had been built by ropes and pots—objects, not people.

Paul banged through the door and tripped, landing hands and knees on the ground. He struggled to his feet and then turned to look back into the bar.

Laughter erupted from the bar behind him and broke over Jamie's back on its way out the door to where Paul still stood looking in, claw-hands balled, and face twisted up.

Jamie knew the old man didn't matter in the grand scheme of things and that he shouldn't have done that, but he felt a relief he hadn't known was possible. Something had been building up. Lots of people had talked shit to him or about him before leading up to fights. They called him slow, they called him stupid, or limited, or predictable, or lucky—which was one he couldn't believe. But then they'd always fought after, and all the anger and anxiety and hopelessness that had built up in Jamie were left in the cage, and when they unlatched the door at the end and he walked down the metal stairs, he left unburdened.

Until he'd thrown Paul to the street, he hadn't realized that things had been building in him for a while now. Since he'd been back. Since before. And he hadn't had any way to get it out of him. That hadn't been much, only a few seconds, and it's not like he'd been able to really struggle against him or anything, but still. He worried that he'd hear about it from Erin, but he did so while drawing breaths in easier and fuller than he had in a while, like there was more room for it in him now.

**WHEN SHE RANG THE BELL** on the wall for last call and then again fifteen minutes later to get everyone moving, those who were still there finished their drinks and filed out with a smile or a nod or a laugh with Jamie as they passed, one or two pausing a second to pose with fists. People had used to do that all the time before or after fights. Men, women, children. He must have taken thousands of photos with strangers' fists pressing against his jaw. Jamie had come in upset, and he still was, mostly, but he couldn't help but smile just a little. Paul was a loser, sure, but it felt great to move with somebody, even someone like that, even just for a second.

He bolted the door when the last of them left, slid into a seat against the wall, and let out a big breath. She joined him. She had a beer in her hand. She didn't bring him a milk.

"I went to that place, earlier," he said. "To the office, what you told me about."

"What the fuck was that with Paul?"

"Oh, same as before. Trying to use me to show off. Now there was an audience."

"No, I mean you. What the fuck was that about with you. You come in here in a shitty mood and then physically throw out a guy who, yeah, is a fucking cunt, but he hadn't actually done anything, had he?"

"Well, he—"

"And do you know why he's always in here? Because he's a thin-skinned little loser who nurses grudges forever. Because every other place in town has eventually gotten fed up with him and told him to fuck off, just once, and he never forgave 'em."

"Well, he was being a real asshole. He—"

"He's a fucking child. You're an adult. And you're being paid to babysit him. We both are."

He just nodded, because he couldn't say anything; for the first time since Japan he felt like he was going to cry—like, really cry—and he couldn't do that in front of anyone.

"God," she continued, "you can't just... Is that what you did in the city? Throw people around just 'cause you don't like 'em?"

Still all he could do was shrug.

"Well, we fucking can't here. We don't have endless fucking people coming through the doors. We don't have endless tries. We're stuck with who we've got, and we've got to make that work or we're fucked."

He could still hear the voices of the drinkers from out in the street, quieter now but still there. He wondered if they had heard her. His face felt hot. But he felt like he could make his voice work without degenerating into a shuddering mess. "Okay. Okay. I get it. So what do we do?"

"I'll get him back. Even though he's got cash, he's a prick, so I'm probably the only one who tolerates him at all. But Jim..."

"I'll behave. I'll buy him a drink."

"Jim, you can't be here."

"What?"

She reached out to grab his hand, but he stood up and walked away from the table.

"So that's it for me just because he spends money?"

She stood up too and followed him, and he paced awkwardly toward the back of the bar, and as she followed him, he felt more and more penned in.

"No, it's because you were wrong. You shouldn't have done that. You made a very expensive mistake. But it was *your* mistake. And you saying that shows you don't get it."

He clenched and unclenched his fists as he paced. He'd give anything to be back in the cage. Not because he wanted to hurt anyone or because he wanted money. But because it was simple, and he understood it. Because he knew how to *be*.

"Earlier I went to this... this fucking... because *you* told me to. And... fuck."

"What? Let's go upstairs," she said.

"Go upstairs? You just told me to get out of here and now you want me to go upstairs."

"I said I can't have you work here anymore, not that I don't want to see you. And be honest, you don't actually want to work here either. You know you don't."

She was talking about those things like they weren't the same, but they were. You were your work. Who you were in the gym was who you were as a person. She was trying to draw lines where there weren't any.

"I'll come down and clean up in the morning," she said. "Let's get out of here and you can tell me what you're talking about."

She reached for his arm, and he slipped away.

"What good's that ever do? Talk, talk, talk. I was trying to talk to Holly Warren today because of what you said and what good did that do? Fuck it."

"Holly Warren?"

He left his sweater on top of the beer in the cold room and went straight to the door. He unbolted it and flung it open, rushing out into the night. And he turned and looked back in through the bouncing door, face hot and twisted up.

SID'S BURSTS OF LAUGHTER RANG out in time with the impacts of Jamie's hammer swings.

"Ease up a bit," he slurred, but he kept right on laughing.

Jamie swung the hammer at the wall that separated the entryway from the living room. He'd come home shaking, hand itching for the hammer as soon as he opened the door. And the ferocity of his assault had drawn Sid out from somewhere, and he'd sat on the stairs resting the big plastic bottle on his knee, and tried to offer instructions, but Jamie just swung over his voice, the impacts shaking the floor beneath him.

They had done fuck all about it since the last time when Sid had left him to clear everything out himself. Jamie'd brought it up a few times since then, but Sid always had some reason he couldn't do it. At first Jamie had thought he just didn't care about it one way or the other, but then he started to think he was actively avoiding it for some reason, drawing the whole thing out, just to fuck with him maybe. Or maybe because he didn't like working with him.

"Want some?" Sid asked. He held up the bottle.

Jamie stopped mid swing, brought the head of the hammer to rest down near his feet. "Yeah."

"Really? Normally I got to force it down you." Sid tilted his head a touch, looked at Jamie almost searchingly.

Jamie held his brother's gaze.

"Alright!" Sid said, jumping from his perch on the stairs and ran to the kitchen. He came back with a tumbler almost full. He handed it to Jamie, and Jamie swallowed it as hard as he could, coughing and spitting all the way. He handed the glass back to his brother, and he nodded. Sid refilled it and Jamie drank half of that and then went and picked up the hammer again.

Sid sat at the base of the stairs and pulled something from his pocket, a crumpled mess of paper. He leafed through it until he found the section he wanted.

"It would have been good to talk to you about some things I think," Sid read. He was doing a voice, like a kid's. "Mo wasn't really a fighter like you and me, so he doesn't get it really sometimes, and I thought you would have got it once you got over it. Well, you don't get over it I guess but get used to it. So it sucked when you left because I thought finally you'd understand, but then you left." Sid held the pages up in the air. "Who the fuck is this loser?" he asked.

It was Robbie's letter. Sid had seen Robbie's writing and read his words. "Why do you have that?" Jamie asked. He tightened his grip on the hammer.

"Saw it sticking out of the thing. Didn't know what it was, so I looked at it and I thought it was funny, so I saved it for you."

"Put it down."

Sid folded the letter up as well as he was able now it was so crumpled and put it on the floor by his feet.

Jamie started swinging, the whisky a hot storm in his stomach.

He sent pieces of drywall and wooden beams flying, arcing up through the air overhead, bouncing off the wall opposite and in one instance punching a small hole in through the living room window.

"What got into you?" Sid asked.

Jamie held the hammer over his shoulder just long enough to speak.

"Fucking Holly Warren."

"Holly Warren? What about her? You remember Mark, with those big-ass teeth. He fucked her. Or he said he did. See, with Mark—"

"No, it's nothing. It's just fucking Erin."

"Erin now? What are you talking about?"

"Nothing." He swung again, and again, and again, until there wasn't much wall left of any kind from the waist up, so he swung low, toward the ground.

The hammer broke through the low wall, then Jamie was on his back in the darkness. He couldn't see. He felt around on the ground near him. For what? Whatever he was looking for, it was the whisky glass he'd set on the ground behind him that he found.

He didn't sit up to drink, he just brought the glass above his lips and poured it in a few drops a time, like he used to do with water when he'd given absolutely everything he had to a session in the gym.

"Alright?" Sid asked.

Jamie grunted.

There weren't streetlights on the road. They'd all been broken or burned out or whatever and there was no town money to fix them.

"Guess there was a wire down that wall after all. Didn't remember." Sid laughed and laughed again, and soon Jamie heard Sid sliding down the rest of the stairs on his butt to the floor along with the sound of his unceasing laughter. And Jamie found himself laughing with him again, laughing and wiggling his fingers to work the shock out of them.

"So the bar didn't work out, eh?" Sid asked eventually.

Jamie drank.

"Gotcha."

"I got something you could do," Sid said.

A car drove past on the street, the headlights momentarily illuminating the room. He saw Sid in the flash, lying beside him on his back, arms at his sides, staring at the ceiling. His skin looked like chalk dust, his eyes blackened.

"What's that? Handywork?"

"Money's great."

"What is it, Sid?"

"I know a guy who moves weight. You know what I'm saying?"

Jamie sat up. "You want me to deal drugs."

"No, no. I know you'd never fucking stoop. But he's got an order coming in and he's a bit short handed and he said if you would agree to just be there for the exchange, he'd make it worth your while. Just one thing. Just between professionals."

"You want me to be a drug dealer."

"That's not what it is."

"I was a fucking world champion."

"Yeah, I know. So great. Flying all over the world. But you're down here on the floor with me. You want to get paid like a world champion again? You can fucking unretire, or you can come with me."

"How the fuck did you get involved in this? What happened to being a handyman?"

He couldn't see his brother in the dark, couldn't feel his voice vibrating through the carpet. He only heard his voice, close but weak, near him in the room but shifting around as if it were spinning around him, or he was. Jamie rubbed his face. The hand felt like it belonged to someone else.

"I was one. I was. But there's no money here. People can't afford much help. And then suddenly I needed the money, and once I started doing that, what real work I had dried up. So that's what I'm stuck with."

"What could have been so fucking important you started dealing?"

"Dad's burial."

Jamie wiggled the tingling from his toes. Another car passed by, another passing flash sent shadows arcing quickly across the room like the time-lapse of a sundial.

"Shit," Jamie said. "You could've just called me. I could have given it to you."

"On what fucking number? Hey? How the fuck was I supposed to do that when you never even called?"

"I called," he said, and then they both went quiet. The only sound was breathing, a few coughs from Sid, and a faint whisper Jamie eventually identified as wind coming in through the hole his hammering had punched through the front window. "I just didn't know what to say."

He lay there a while longer until it was clear neither of them knew what to say then either, and then he got onto his hands and knees—he didn't think he could walk right anymore, and he couldn't see shit besides—and crawled up to bed.

Jamie hung his spinning head out his window in search of cool air and moonlight and thought of when he'd first gone to sleep above the gym. He wasn't yet comfortable there and couldn't sleep. He'd get up and walk around and check to make sure everything was alright, Robbie would appear and talk to him and give him things to do, cleaning jobs or training drills, or just talk to him, tell him dumb stories until his eyelids grew too heavy to keep casting scared glances into corners and the space between the heavy bags.

## Age Twenty-Eight
That short doctor knelt in front of him in their little, curtained-off hallway examination area somewhere in the guts of the stadium. He said things to Jamie in Japanese, but the language didn't matter because Jamie's ears were ringing, and he couldn't hear anyway. He kept shining a penlight in his eyes, and Jamie kept shying away from it and trying to say he was fine.

The doctor sprang to his feet and bent over his wheeled trolley, his back to Jamie, and scribbled on some paperwork that waited on top of it.

From somewhere nearby he heard Mo's voice, and Robbie's dull bass, and he heard Meg—Megumi—their chaperone, alternating English and Japanese, but he could not understand what any of them were saying.

He breathed out and struggled to his feet and groaned, favouring his right knee. The doctor was writing something on a clipboard, and Jamie limped out from behind the sheets or curtains or whatever they were. His team was down the hall to his right, talking with some promoters. He went left.

There seemed to be a wind running through this hallway, but he was grateful for it; he radiated heat—he could feel the steam rising up from his chest and hitting his glowing cheeks—and that fight had taken so much out of him he'd stopped sweating in the third round, though he was still slick and sticky with it.

He walked until the halls grew empty and he saw an open dressing room door and went in. There were blue mats spread across the floor, but they'd been pushed askew by use and were streaked in places by sweat. There were folding chairs scattered around the room and tape and cotton from hand wraps scattered around the floor. Whoever had used this room had packed up and gone.

He sat in one of the chairs and hunched forward, picked a discarded towel up from the floor and hung it over his head and pulled at the Velcro wrist strap of his gloves with his teeth. His mouth was a desert—it was hard to even open it—his tongue and cheeks and the roof of his mouth all rough like sand.

He wedged a couple fingers of his left hand into the glove and wrenched it off. Then he ripped the Velcro off the other glove with his teeth and tried to remove his left the same way, but the pain coming up in his hand was too much.

He sat there, hunched over, towel covering his head, his hand throbbing with each heartbeat and his skin clammy and his mouth desiccated. And he cried, the tears he was unsure he could even physically produce at that point flowed free and hot and stupid down his face and mixed on the floor with the pooling sweat—some his, some the strangers whose space he was taking up.

He didn't know how long he sat there and wept, but at some point he heard muffled voices in the hallway and the intermittent sound of doors being thrown open.

He pressed the towel up against his face, and his door flung open then, smacking into the hard doorstop with a bang, and Robbie appeared in the empty space.

"Finally," he shouted, and he leaned back out the door and called for Mo and stepped in, and Jamie heard Mo's stubby legs pound down the hall toward him.

"Jamie," Mo said when he crashed in. He sounded angry, upset.

"It's just sweat," Jamie said. He wiped his face again with the towel.

"Boy, what are you doing here? Whose room is this?" Mo cast a searching gaze around the room for clues.

"Sorry."

"Well, no problem. Doc wants to see you again though. To be sure."

"Sorry."

"Yeah, well."

"I'm so sorry." He couldn't stop himself from saying it.

"Wait, why you sorry?"

Jamie shook his head. He shut his eyes.

"The fight?" Mo shouted. "The fight, boy? Jesuuuuus."

And suddenly Mo's arms were around him and he lifted him, and Jamie's weight came off the ground until only his toes half rested there.

"Apologize for that fight, boy? Crazy. Don't. Don't you dare," Mo said into Jamie's chest. "Shut up, boy, it's okay."

At some point Jamie became aware of Robbie's hand messing his hair, patting him gently on the back, and Mo kept telling him it was okay.

Jamie couldn't open his eyes, but even as tightly closed as they were, almost of their own accord, they could still not keep the tears in when they came again.

**JAMIE WANTED TO SPEND THE** night in the hotel room as he often did after his fights, but Meg had arranged for a sponsored appearance at a sports bar, and he'd have to return the money, however much it was, if he didn't go. He didn't know how long it would be before he could fight again, so he couldn't afford that. So he showered and pissed blood and got dressed in a big, shiny collared shirt Robbie had helped him pick out, and after he put on a splint he'd saved from the last time he'd broken his hand, they went down to the lobby to wait.

Meg was the star student of a friend and former trainer of Mo's, Han, whose gym they trained at while Jamie had got over his jetlag, and she escorted them around the city and got them settled in and acted as their translator.

Meg had refused to train with him, and, from what Jamie had seen in the gym, any men at all. But she had been incredibly polite to him otherwise, and he was secretly a little glad for her refusal. Despite being barely more than half his weight, there was something about her, a perfect confidence that terrified him in the gym and he feared would have made him fold.

But outside the gym it was compelling, and when she walked through the lobby doors, he felt himself almost, for a second, excited.

"Are you sure this is still on?" Jamie asked.

"Still on?" she repeated.

"Like, they still want to do this? They still want me to come?"

"Yes. Why?"

"I lost."

"No, no it's good," she said, and she ushered them into the waiting car.

Inside, she said, "Congratulations."

He swallowed.

They stopped in a square about a ten-minute ride from the hotel, though with traffic it did not seem like they had gone very far at all and they might almost have been able to walk the distance in the same time.

The street was densely packed, and all the buildings went up, like, straight up, high, and even though he'd been living in the city a while now it still made him a little dizzy.

They went into what looked more like an office building than anything. They took the elevator up twelve floors with a dozen other men, and he was a half a head taller than all of them except Robbie.

The bar itself didn't look "Japanese" in any way he expected, though now he couldn't think of what way that was. They played the same pop music he'd heard over the gym radio back home and the neon signs behind the bar were all in English for western beers and the framed team jerseys on the wall were for western teams, and they had the same uncomfortable stools around high tables they had in the bar just down the road from his house.

One man, who sat in the bench seats against the far wall, was clearly asleep. But otherwise everyone looked happy and professional and most people wore suits or other nice clothes. Meg looked right at home. She wore a tailored black suit and a white shirt and had short hair that barely touched her neck, and it was slicked back.

She sat them down in a roped-off booth and disappeared. Jamie sat as far back as he could, tucked himself into one of the booth's corners. The televisions showed an after show—his fights back home never had after shows—with suited men and women talking about the event just passed, interspersed with slow-motion clips of the fights themselves.

Soon Meg came back with a box in each hand, followed by a waitress with a tray of drinks. She put the boxes on the end of the table. They were short and squat, and the bottle that Robbie quickly pulled out was too. It was round and ridged and had a sort of bulbous stopper for the lid—it looked like one of those crystal containers rich people kept their old whisky or cognac in. The label looked expensive and it had that nice Japanese writing on it that overall was sort of shaped like a tree.

"Oh, we didn't order this," Jamie said, and then to Mo, he said, "This stuff looks expensive, and...no win bonus."

"No, no," Meg said. "From the bar. For you."

"There must be some mistake," Jamie said. "Robbie..." He waved his hand at him.

"No, no. For you. For your fight."

"Well, I mean—Robbie, put it back—I lost. They must have thought I won. And if we open it and they realize that I lost, they'll take it out of my appearance fee and then..."

He'd seen how people treated losers back home.

"No," she said. She smiled at him. "They know. They watched. Everybody watched. They loved it."

"I lost."

"The Japanese don't care as much about win or lose. You fought great. Look." She pointed out behind her to the room full of people, who had become aware of his presence and were casting furtive, anticipatory glances his way.

"Great show. They loved it. They loved you."

Meg nodded and leaned forward and patted him on the arm. She must not have been paying much attention because she brought her hand down on his splint, but he didn't feel it. Everyone was smiling at him.

She strolled off again and Jamie looked at Robbie who squinted and looked pointedly out the window.

"Sorry, Robbie."

"S'fine."

"No, I am sorry. Really."

"S'fine."

"Serious. That bottle you wouldn't get your mitts off? That's yours. Take it. Please."

Robbie held out for a few seconds before he smiled and turned back and grabbed the bottle up again, turning it in his hands and holding it up to the light.

Meg came back with four glasses and sat at the edge of the booth.

"Open the other up for us, will ya, Mo?" Jamie said.

Mo opened a bottle and poured out three drinks, but when he reached for the fourth glass, he saw that Robbie had already taken it.

"It's alright. I've got my own," he said through a smile so un-self-conscious Jamie's cheeks were sore just looking at it. Or they would be if he hadn't taken a bunch of pain killers. Robbie opened the bottle Jamie had just given him and poured himself a small measure and then looked back at the bottle, eying up how much was gone from it, smiling the whole time.

They all held up their glasses and toasted Jamie. He took a sip and nearly choked. "Jesus, it's like fire!" He looked around to see if the others felt the same. Robbie stared down at it. Meg had her eyes closed. Mo held it up to the light.

Jamie dried his chin with the splint. "Probably shouldn't have any more because of the pain killers. It's great, though."

Meg started waving fans over to the booth. The first man approached wearing a track jacket and a baseball cap with expensive looking jeans and shoes, all the clothes without wrinkle or blemish.

Jamie had expected everyone to bow deep at the waist like they did in the movies he watched as a kid, but it was more like they nodded. It reminded Jamie of the slight head incline that two men will give each other when passing in the street that says *I see you*.

The man handed Jamie a plastic bag, the inside dewed a bit with condensation, filled with several paper bags folded over at the tops. "Mac burger," the guy said. "For you." And then he said some more things in Japanese and gestured to Jamie and the rest at the table.

No one had ever bought him food after a fight before and, honestly, he wouldn't have trusted it if they did, but for some reason it seemed fine here, so he took the bag and put it on the table and Robbie dove right in.

"Thank you," Jamie said, but he didn't know if he understood him, so he looked at Meg and said thank you to her to translate, but then he felt rude, so he looked back at the gentleman and thanked him again. Through Meg, the guy, whose name was Kaito, asked him about Tamura, if he had ever been to Japan before, and how he felt about the Japanese crowd. And Jamie responded through Meg that Tamura was tough and had a bright future, but he couldn't be more specific because he couldn't really remember the fight actually, and Japan seemed nice, but he hadn't had a chance to do much yet except train and fight.

And when he tried to answer how he felt about the Japanese crowd, he thought about the eerie, pin-drop silence that had filled the stadium during the fight, which he'd been told ahead of time was a sign of respect, and then the enormous response afterwards, and the gifts of whisky and food and Kaito's nod and sheepish smile and the line-up of nodding people behind him, and all Jamie could do was smile at Meg and nod to her and stumble over his tongue trying to remember what Mo had taught him for thank you in Japanese. And then he stood for the standard fighter-fan photo, the two of them facing off with fists raised in a mock showdown. And then Kaito bowed again, deeper, and left, and Jamie waited for the next person to approach.

They came with gifts and questions for the rest of the night. But as the pain started to come back to him he found it harder and harder to answer the questions, even through Meg. Sometimes his head hurt so much he would lose track of what Meg was saying while she was saying it, even though her English was better than his probably. Sometimes when someone left the table and no one else was waiting straight away, he still couldn't sit down for a minute because his back had seized up. Sometimes people would ask questions and he couldn't answer with anything more than a nod or a curl of the corners of his mouth because his hand hurt so much that to open his mouth would be to groan or cry. But he stood there at the end of the booth, meeting and posing for a showdown with what seemed like every single person that walked through those doors until almost four in the morning when the sun had begun to make its comeback.

Meg dropped them at the front door of the hotel and the three of them rode the elevator up in silence. In the hallway, Jamie hugged them both.

"Just wait till next time, boy," Mo said.

"Yeah, Champ. You'll get him next time."

They all went to their rooms, and Jamie walked across to the window in the dim, grey light of the dawn and looked out over the city and wiped at his eyes with his splint.

# Chapter 8

THE DOOR WASN'T THE BIG, double job out front you went through on your way to meet God. It was a little steel door down a flight of rain-slick steps tucked away out of view that led into the church basement. There were a couple people smoking at the top of the stairs. They looked at Jamie as he walked past. He looked at the ground, clutching a single crumpled piece of paper in his hand. The door squealed a bit when he opened it.

It smelled damp in there. He could hear feet. It was low ceilinged with fluorescent lighting that made everyone and everything look bleached. The flooring was a dark tan and grey laminate. There were thin-legged tables and chairs stacked up against the far wall.

In the middle were about a half-dozen kids of various ages—maybe six to twelve, but he'd never really spent much time around kids, so he didn't know—each clad head to toe in white canvas pajamas of varying levels of dustiness.

A man approached him, also *gi*-ed up. His *gi* was more broken in—or worn out—and the limp black belt at his waist contained him a little less well. He was taller than Jamie, older, skinnier in the arms and legs, and pot-bellied. He was in good shape for just a guy, Jamie figured, but not for an athlete. His hair was buzzed to the scalp.

"What can I do for you?" he asked.

"Just looking to... just seeing what's on offer. What's going on."

"Ah, okay. Well, this is pretty much it. It's mostly just kids, but I do have some men and women come through occasionally. Us old guys have to stay in shape somehow, you know?" He laughed and elbowed Jamie in the ribs.

"Yeah, I know."

"So what do you think? You want to join us? It's two sessions a week for ten bucks. I'm Peter, by the way."

Across the room, a blond boy ran up behind another, taller boy and tried to kick him in the head, but his bare feet slipped on the lino and he landed on his back.

"Hi, Peter. I actually wondered if maybe you'd need some help, or something."

"Oh, you've got experience in karate?"

"Not karate in particular. Other martial arts though. Boxing, kickboxing, judo, jiu jitsu, wrestling."

"Wow. Okay. With kids?"

"No, but I like kids, you know? I think so. I'd like to. I'd like to spend more time with kids, I think."

"Ah," the guy said. He shifted to the side a bit to stand directly in between Jamie and the bulk of the children. He looked over at where the blond boy was pulling himself up off the floor. "Good work, Marcus." He turned his attention back to Jamie. "Well, there's really just me and like, half a dozen kids. We could talk more if you want, see what you know, but there's no money in it. No one in this town can afford anything."

Jamie nodded.

"What's your name?"

"Jamie Stuart."

"Stuart... Stuart... as in?"

Jamie nodded, lined the inside of his shoe up against the

edge of a square on the flooring. "Yeah. My dad. Or brother, I guess, depending."

"Huh," Peter said. He shuffled a little more squarely in between Jamie and the kids. "Well, nothing here at the moment, but you could leave your info, if you want. I'll... uh, let you know if anything... comes up."

"Right," Jamie said.

His phone had been disconnected a few days earlier. There wasn't any money left in his account to pay for it. And he was actually relieved by that a bit because that meant Doctor Carroll wouldn't call and leave him messages anymore about wanting to know if he was okay, and if he wanted to come back in to work or just to talk, and he wouldn't freeze at the sound of the ringer, and then feel embarrassed like a scorned child after the ring died out, and drink a few drinks to deal with the embarrassment.

"No," Jamie continued. "My contract ran out. I'm looking for better rates. So I thought I'd come by. But it's alright. I don't really have any karate, like you said."

As he left the gym, the sound of the kids' feet squeaking on the tile played him out. Maybe he wasn't ready to be a real coach, not after what had happened the last time. But he thought this was so far away from actual fighting that maybe he could still have done it without repeating what he did. The people were gone from outside. When he passed over the pile of dead and dying cigarette butts they'd left on the sidewalk, he dropped the piece of paper he'd been clutching down onto the ground with them. It had the silhouette of a strong, muscled man on it and read "Martial Arts—for fitness, confidence, discipline."

**SOMEONE ELSE USED TO DO** it for him, but now he didn't have anybody else. He tried to do it just like he was used to, sitting the wrong way around with his arms resting across the back of a chair in the belly of an arena somewhere. Normally the chair was the metal folding kind with a flat top, but this was wood with a high, curved back, which got in his way and made it more difficult. And it was in the dining room. But it was as close as he was able to get.

He struggled at it that way a while before he spun the right way around in his chair and unravelled the yellow wraps from his hands onto the floor and started again. He pinched one end of the wrap between his thumb and the third knuckle on his index finger. There was a loop at the end of the wrap you were meant to slide over the thumb, but that's not how he'd learned. When Mo had learned, they hadn't had the professional, western-style wraps with the thumb loops. They'd just used rolls of gauze or linen, and that's how he'd taught Jamie and that's how Jamie did it now.

He wrapped it broad-ways around the knuckle three times, each time tugging it tight, and then started bringing the wrap down in between his fingers instead of around the outside of his hand on alternating passes. When he'd worked all the way in from his pinkie, he began to work his way down his hand and wrist until the long cotton wrap—one hundred and eighty inches; fifteen feet; four and a half metres—provided protection to his knuckles, support to his hand, and stability to the wrist, and then fastened it with a Velcro strip at the end.

And then he did the same for his other hand. For the first time in months, it felt like his hands, wrapped as they were, belonged to him. He hadn't noticed how unlike himself he'd been feeling until he reintroduced himself to the routine of being Jamie, the King.

When he was wrapped up, he slipped on his shoes and ran out onto the street, forcing himself to run. It wasn't as easy as it used to be, but a little easier than it had been lately. He had something that resembled a goal. He ran about a mile and a half up and down the streets near to his house—slow and heavy footed, but he did it.

When he got what counted for his second wind these days, he returned home and walked through to the back garden, grabbing his training gloves from the kitchen counter on the way. He'd kept them with him this whole time, lugged them across half the country. He pushed his hand into one glove and used his teeth to drag on the second. That feeling made his shoulders, and his whole body soon after, go tight, but not like a knot—like a spring. He was ready. As ready as he'd been in a while. As ready as he was gonna get. There wasn't anything for him here, he knew now. No job at the hospital, no job at the bar, not even coaching kids in their stupid karate. Things were weird now with the doctor, and with Erin too. It would be better for him, for everyone, if he could just go back to where he belonged. So he'd see if he could. He'd see if he could become himself again. One last try. And if he couldn't... well, then he'd have to see what else was left for him to become.

People always thought gloves were to protect your opponent, to take some of the sting off the punches, but it's the opposite. Gloves protect the hands, allowing you to hit harder. His hand had been feeling better each week he'd been back—except for that first night when he'd gotten drunk and swung without wrapping up first. His hand had been getting better, and everything else here had been getting worse. He had to see if he could finally swap out one for the other. Maybe the doc had been wrong. That's always the story you read about, the million to one chance that comes through—the once-paralyzed woman who walks down the aisle on her wedding day. The injured fighter who comes back stronger than ever.

The bag was swinging a little in the wind and he swung with it, just followed it with his feet, moved in after it, slid out of its way, circled around it, for a long while before he threw his first punch—a left hook. It felt good, natural. He circled around when it swung back around to him and fired two more quick left hooks. And then he slid a little farther out and started working his jab, slipping his head down off the centre line, keeping the bag at a distance, preventing it from getting too close, keeping it frustrated.

When he had his movement down and he was comfortable with the rhythm, he started to feel an itch in his right arm. It started in the shoulder. Every time he'd circle around or corral the bag into the right spot, his arm would twitch, half firing on instinct, on desire.

And finally, after working his left for about ten minutes, the bag came right at him, and he circled out of the way just perfectly, and fired a hard left hook into the middle of it, folding it over and stopping its progress, and when it shook there, almost stunned, on the end of the chain, he followed up with a beautiful right cross.

He felt a twinge—but it wasn't too bad. It might not have been anything to do with a break. It might just have been his hand waking up. Coming back to life. Of course that would not be a painless process. Babies came into the world screaming. His hand, reborn, would be the same.

He worked the bag two handed for... he didn't know how long. He moved out there without time, outside of time. At once he was back at Mo's, gliding in the faint glow of the growing dawn through the forest of heavy bags; he was in his first official fight and taking a clean right to the face and realizing that he could take it, that it was nothing nearly as bad as what he'd already taken from his dad; back in that first round against Tamura, feeling everything come together on the big stage, before it all went to shit.

He worked a few elbows and knees, some push kicks and low kicks—he never really had the flexibility or the style to land much above the elbow—but he threw those mostly out of a sense of obligation. The joy of this day came from his right hand, from the feeling of something lost having come home. He worked short uppercuts and one-two combos, alternating hooks and once, when he was feeling almost too loose, a spinning backfist that missed and sent him stumbling, then laughing.

And through the whole ordeal, the pain in his hand grew fainter, dimmer, until it disappeared altogether. Some sensation disappeared with it. He didn't feel that perfect pop of the impact as clearly as he should have, but the important part was there was no pain. It was really holding up. He smiled. If his hand was better, he could fight again. The doc would see that she'd been wrong about it. Erin, Holly. He wouldn't have to consider Sid's plan anymore. He wouldn't be stuck with nothing.

When it was done, when his arms were so heavy he couldn't reset them to his chin, when his punches were looping or drooping and lazy, and the back of his gloves dripped with the sweat he'd wiped off his brow, he sat down with his back against the wall and watched the bag swing with the echoes of that moment, the swings getting smaller and smaller until the bag hung still, until there was no trace at all of what Jamie'd just done.

He pulled his gloves off by pinching them in his armpits. He held up his right hand. It looked fine. He tried to flex it, to make a good strong fist, but it didn't really respond. It was slow and weak. He ripped open the Velcro strip of his hand wrap and started unravelling the yellow length of cotton, up from the wrist to his hand, to his knuckles. As the wrap loosened, it seemed to let the pain in, the feeling of fire creeping farther up as he peeled his hand free. When he'd shaken the whole thing off his hand throbbed with each heartbeat.

The skin was white when he freed it, with thin red lines cut in, but it wasn't long before it started to glow. At first a bright red, and then it grew deeper. He tried to peel the Velcro off the other side, but his hand was already too stiff and lazy. He couldn't squeeze tight enough. The strap just kept slipping from his grasp.

He tore it off with his teeth and then went back into the kitchen, leaving the gloves and wraps on the ground. Sid had bought a small bag of ice earlier and left it in the sink. His brother hadn't gotten around to fixing the power after his demolition accident, and Jamie didn't know how to, so they lost everything in the fridge and freezer and now only bought things if they were going to eat them all that day.

"How'd it go?" Sid shouted from the other room. "Your triumphant return." Then he walked over and leaned coolly against the door frame.

Jamie grabbed the ice and poured it into a jug or a wide mouth vase or whatever it was that Sid had sitting empty on the counter and pressed his hand down into it. It was a dark red and it had already begun to balloon up so much he wouldn't have been able to get the gloves back on. The throbbing had worked its way up his arm and was stabbing into the base of his neck. He was done. He knew it. He wasn't going to be staging a comeback. He'd known a while, he thought, deep down, but this was the first time he'd ever really admitted it to himself. But even so, even if this only confirmed his long-held suspicions, he couldn't cope with it all now. Not so recent. Not with his hand throbbing and Sid waiting. The only thing he could do right this second was move on.

"Your guy still need extra hands?" Jamie asked. He could grieve later.

"You even got a pair to offer at this point?"

"I got one and the promise of another."

Sid walked into the kitchen. He laughed at Jamie's hand in the jug. "My old lady used to keep petunias in there. You're a petunia now, eh?"

Jamie held the jug to his chest, looked back out the back door. He wanted to ask his brother about his old lady. Sid's daughter's mother, he assumed. He wanted to know everything about her. Who was she, what she was like? Did he miss her?

And what had Sid been like with her? It was hard to picture his brother holding a bundle of flowers he'd bought or holding her hand, gentle and warm. He couldn't see him with anything in his hand but the neck of a whisky bottle or the handle of a hammer or the anger of a balled fist. But he must have been like that at one point, surely. He must even be like that now, in some way. He wanted to see that side of him, but he didn't know how to. He wanted to know about who his brother had been when Jamie was away, but he couldn't just ask. It was all too much.

"Petunias, huh?"

"Yeah."

"So does he, or not?" Jamie said.

"Probably."

"Then I'll do it, I guess."

Sid squinted. "Why?"

"Nothing else I can do."

"No going back with this," he said. He stepped forward. His face was as earnest as Jamie had ever seen it, had that same look he'd had all those years ago when they separated in the countryside, that look of being drawn toward something he didn't want but couldn't avoid.

"What else have I got?"

"I mean it. In is in. You don't get to decide later that it's not for you."

Jamie looked down at his hand, then up at his brother. He shrugged.

"Well then." Sid nodded back. He pulled Jamie's jug away from his chest and put it in the sink, fist still ensconced. He picked a bottle of Worthy's from the counter, spun the cap off onto the floor, and upended it into the jug.

It stung Jamie's nostrils and his knuckles, where it must have been finding its way into a few small cuts or scrapes he'd gotten from the bag work. Used to be that he could go for hours without so much as a little blush against the bone.

Jamie tried to pull his fist out, but Sid grabbed him by the elbow. "I'm not precious. And there's no more ice so it'll have to do double duty, recovery and celebration."

"Celebration. Yeah."

"Stuart brothers, together again."

Sid angled Jamie's arm a little and the jug a lot until he poured two quarter pints of whisky, ice, and glove sweat into two glasses and handed Jamie one.

"Why are you so sure there's no changing my mind?"

Sid took a long drink. "Tried it once. Wendy—Wendy's my ex's name. I ever tell you that? Eventually Wendy couldn't be convinced anymore that I wasn't doing what I was doing and started talking about going to her sister's house with Mary."

"Mary?" Jamie said. He felt like he needed to sit down.

"Yeah." Sid finished his drink. Jamie surprised himself by doing the same thing and he took his hand out of the jug and dripped onto the kitchen floor while he refilled them.

"You named her Mary."

"Yeah. Thought you'd like that. Anyway, I met Wendy and she got pregnant and we rented a house 'cause Dad was real bad then—"

"Then . . ." Jamie said.

Sid ignored him. "And I didn't want her in here, and things were good a while. And she had the kid and I started doing a bit of, uh, side work, because kids are expensive and money's real tight down here, and she caught on pretty quick and told me to cut it out or fuck off so I cut it out. So we're scraping by and then out of nowhere Dad totally dried out. Didn't think he could have, but he did."

"Yeah, I heard that before," Jamie scoffed.

"What?" Sid squinted at him.

"Nothing," Jamie said quickly. "It's bullshit."

"Well, it's true," Sid said. "Swear on Mom's grave. Had a rough week and then he was good. He was helpful and he met Mary a couple times and he was good with her."

"He didn't," Jamie said.

"He did," Sid said. He wrenched the window open and leaned across the counter onto the windowsill and looked away from Jamie as he talked. He fished a smoke from his pocket almost as an afterthought.

"It's bullshit," Jamie said. He needed it to be.

"It's not," he said. "But then one morning, Dad's floating in the harbour and I got nothing to pay for all his funeral with, and lawyers and whatever, so I go back to the side work. What else could I do? We moved in here and when I'd paid off all the burial and funeral expenses and everything, I told them I was gonna quit cause the old lady didn't like me doing it, and the boss set his Nazi-Frankenstein-looking motherfucker on me and Wendy found me the next morning leaned up against the front door, bleeding out of pretty much every hole I got and a few they'd made just for me. Took me over a month to heal up. By that time Wendy and Mary were long gone. And if I ever had a chance of getting real work again it went away when I went around town looking like that. Everyone knew what I'd been doing, so then that was all I could do. And I got to do something—got to pay for the kid."

"I...I had no idea."

"Yeah. How could you? I didn't exactly want you to. It's not something I'm proud of."

They both finished their drinks and refilled them and he hung his whisky-soaked fist above the kitchen floor and the air hit it and it felt like an arctic wind and drops ran from his knuckle like tears or rain off the roof of a hollowed-out old shell of a building.

"Nazi Frankenstein?" he asked. The rest was all too much to ask about.

"Some Lurch-looking, white-power asshole my boss has around sometimes. Used to fight in prison or something. I don't know. But he's tough as shit, and if I was any drunker than I was when he found me, my body might have been a lot colder come morning, if you know what I mean."

He pictured Sid folded up against the wall, bruised and beaten for his wife to find him. Or girlfriend. He still didn't know. When he was twelve, he'd found Sid in a similar position once after getting into it with his dad, lying in that clawfoot bathtub, leg hooked over the side, bleeding down the drain. In both pictures of Sid, the imagined one and the remembered one, he looked fourteen. Jamie wanted to track this guy down right now and beat him to death. He felt out of his comfort zone in pretty much every interaction he'd had since coming back to this town, but the idea of going and kicking this shit out of some Nazi tough guy called out to him with its siren song of clarity. That's the type of problem he knew how to solve.

But his hand wouldn't hold up. And where would they be then? And Sid was an adult. He'd been working things out for himself since Jamie had left. Since before that, even. He couldn't just act for them both. But he could ask. He could give him the opportunity to say yes.

"If you don't want to do it, I can go with you to tell them. I'm here now. I can handle some brawler."

Sid let out a sympathetic sigh. "You sure?" he said, and inclined his head to Jamie's hand, and Jamie suddenly remembered how much it hurt and put it back into the whisky jug. "This is fine though," Sid said. "Second best thing, my brother out there with me. Second best is alright, right? The silver medal." He poured himself more drinks—straight from the bottle, not bothering with the jug anymore, and always offered

Jamie one as well, and Jamie didn't always refuse. Sid laughed and shadow boxed and pretended to fight him, and Jamie stood cooling his fist in the whisky, stewing in it.

HE'D BEEN DRUNK FOR TWO straight days and wanted to keep being drunk, but he sobered up just to get this one thing done. The door opened harder than it used to. It felt more reluctant. He shouldered through it. The Anchor was as busy as he'd expected, the faces mostly familiar. There was no one on the door. Erin was behind the bar. She clocked him the moment he walked in, her face unmoving. Not unhappy, necessarily, just unreadable. But her eyes flashed instantly to the lump at the centre of the bar. She'd successfully wooed Paul back.

Jamie walked up behind him. Paul dropped one of his stubby legs on the floor and moved to stand up. Jamie fastened him to his seat with one hand on his shoulder. The others leaned away from him. He didn't know if it was because they were afraid or because he'd done a lot of drinking and no showering since he'd had the conversation in the kitchen with Sid.

He looked over the man's head to Erin. He nodded. The corners of her lips flickered up, just for a second. They were nice lips. She hadn't told him to get out yet. He'd wanted to call her after he left last time to apologize once he'd calmed down, and he'd wanted to call earlier when he'd had this idea, but his phone had been cut off so he had just had to hope for the best.

"How much for the whisky?" he said.

She raised an eyebrow. "You know how much."

"The Nikashi, I mean."

The men at the bar were still silent, but they cast a few sly looks to one another.

"Don't know, I've never actually... seven fifty."

"For the whole bottle, I mean. I've got one sixty." He took his hand off Paul's shoulder and dug two weekends worth of work out of his pocket.

She took it, but still froze a beat before she slid it into the till. "Why the hell not?" she said. "Nobody else fucking wants it." She pulled the bottle down and extended it to him.

He nodded down to the bar. "And glasses for Paul and his friends. Not for me."

She slid out some glasses and poured out the Nikashi. "Sure you don't want in on this? You bought it," she said.

"I've had my share. And that's all the cash I've got."

She poured him a double Worthy's and gave it to him with a wink. He took a seat against the wall opposite and watched Erin behind the bar and listened to the men talk shit and cough over the much stronger, heavier drink than they were used to. Colin turned and raised his glass.

Paul still sat and chatted shit, but it was different now. His back hunched lower. His voice was quieter. He passed by some opportunities to be an asshole, and the ones he seized got less of a response than they might have used to. Jamie didn't know when the old man had been in his prime, but those days were obviously long past. It was alright to be real about who you'd become, right? They all needed that.

He drank as many Worthy's as she poured him.

An hour or so later they poured out the last of the Nikashi and Jamie rose on loose legs and collected the empty bottle from the bar. He forced a quick smile to Erin. He felt it disappear almost as quickly as it came. She nodded.

"Do you want to come up later and talk?" she said. "Not tonight obviously. You're shitfaced. But sometime."

He smiled. "Sure. Sometime."

He sat back on his own against the wall and turned the bottle over in his hand. It didn't look that impressive in this light. Empty. He lay it out on its side on the table and watched as it slowly rolled over, eventually falling from the table and coming to rest in the darkness under the seat.

## Age Thirty

This kid kept dropping his right when he doubled up on his jab, even after he'd been told.

"Don't do that, Jack," Jamie said. "I've seen him. He's got a hook."

"Yes, Coach." The kid bobbed his head in a nod, and several drops of sweat fell from his brow and darkened the mats beneath them.

"Don't 'Coach' me. Mo's your coach. And Robbie. I'm just trying to help you not get knocked out while I've got time between fights."

"Thanks, Coach," the kid said. And he fired a double jab again, and then again, pounding it into the black leather of the heavy bag.

"You can thank me by not dropping your hand," Jamie said.

The kid shook his head, angry at himself. Jamie shook his head too. The kid pumped that double jab again, and again, still doing it, still dropping that right. He never did it when shadow boxing, only when he was landing on something solid, a bag or a man. It was like he was attempting to push through the resistance, and that made him tuck his right arm down against his chest.

Jamie smiled, and said, "Don't worry. We'll get you there."

He left the kid there to work it out on the bag, and went to the office to see Mo. The kid watched him as he walked away; Jamie could tell, because he didn't hear the jab anymore or the accompanying breaths.

After he had come back from Japan, he'd noticed a lot of people would watch him. He'd come in to see Mo or help prep one of his teammates for an upcoming bout, and he'd feel the eyes on him. No one wanted to bother him, but he held their attention.

But in the ten months since—as that fight faded some from people's minds, and there was no news of a new booking, and Jamie spent more time hanging off the ropes shouting instructions than inside the ring doing the work—it was happening less and less. Few people, other than Jack who couldn't jab, seemed interested in him anymore.

It was like with lions; when they're in their prime, everyone in the pride pays attention to them, to their mood, their location, their actions. When the pride stops respecting them so much, it's a sign a challenge is coming, that they're about to be driven out by a younger, hungrier, less diseased challenger. He sometimes felt like the vultures were already circling him, even though he was as strong now as he'd ever been. He could lift more than ever.

Mo was in his office on his laptop, probably playing poker. Jamie sat down across from him.

"Hey, Champ. Hey. How's the kid out there?"

"Won't quit dropping his right. Gonna get laid out if he keeps it up."

"He'll get it."

"I'm worried he won't have time to get it."

"Then he'll get knocked out. Then he'll learn."

"And you're okay with that? So he can end up like Robbie?"

"Hey, now. Robbie... Well, anyway, he's an adult. This is what he wants."

"He's a kid. He doesn't know what he wants."

"Neither did you. But I knew for you."

Jamie ran his hand through his hair. "Any news from Honor?"

"They'll book you when you want to get booked. But no point, with your hand. Won't even make it through training camp."

"I talked to Doc Webb this morning."

"And?"

"He's not pleased with it. He wants me to come in for another meeting about having another surgery."

"Okay."

"Okay, Mo? Another surgery?"

"If you need it, you need it. What you going to do, not get it?" He shrugged again. "There we are."

There was a knock on the door and Robbie walked in. He stood behind Jamie and put his hands on his shoulders and started to massage him. "Ready to go train the kid, Champ? Me and you'll turn him into a beast."

Jamie shrugged his shoulders away. "Jesus, Robbie, we're talking here."

Robbie pulled his hands back, tucked them under his armpits. "Sorry."

"Speaking of talking, I, uh, also got a phone call today," Mo said.

"Oh, yeah?" Jamie leaned forward.

Mo hissed a breath in through clenched teeth, as if he'd just had salt rubbed into a wound. "Kage Killers is stripping you."

"What?" Jamie stood up and his legs shoved the chair out behind him. He'd been with Kage Killers for years. Years and years. He had not seen this coming. Had not allowed himself to.

"They said you could probably fight for it if you ever come back. But counting the time you took off to fight for Honor, and the time that you've been off since... Been almost two years, Champ. Well over. It's in your contract. A year of inactivity."

"I've been fucking recovering."

"The contract, Jamie."

"It's my fucking belt, Mo. It's mine. I own it. I paid for it with my fucking hand." Jamie staggered back and slumped into the chair.

Mo's desk phone rang and he held his index finger up and said, "One second" and he answered it. "Hello?"

His eyes snapped up to meet Jamie's, and he tilted his head. "Yes," he said. "Alright, one second then." He held the receiver out to Jamie. The curly cord swung and knocked over his pen cup.

"Who is it? Kage Killers want to give me my fucking belt back?"

"I don't know who. Just for you. Some guy. And since you're already here, why not?"

Jamie placed the receiver to his ear. It was already warm from its brief time against Mo's head.

"Hello?"

"Jamie?" the voice said.

"Yeah, who's this?"

"Jamie," the voice said again. His father.

"What the fuck do you want?" Jamie said.

There was a long silence on the phone. "Your brother. He's having a bit of...trouble."

"So help him."

"I am," he said. His father's voice was so much thinner than Jamie remembered. "I'm trying to. But I'm not sure—"

"Might be easier if you dry out."

"I am," he said. "I'm trying to."

Jamie stood up and stepped toward the door, but the cord pulled tight and dragged the base of the phone across Mo's desk and toward the edge, sending papers and stationery to the floor.

"What do you want me to do?"

"Come home. Not forever, I mean. But to see him. Just for a bit."

"Home. Right." Jamie laughed. "Listen, I...this isn't a great time for me."

Mo and Robbie stared at him, and then at each other when he gave them nothing. Mo raised an eyebrow. Robbie stepped forward, as if to be in place in case he needed to step in.

"It's not a great time for anyone," his father said.

Jamie walked back to the desk and slammed the phone down in the cradle and slammed himself down into the chair. He swiped the phone off the table and it clattered down onto the floor.

Mo picked up the phone and held the phone to his ear to see if it was broken. "You okay, boy?"

"Fine. Just my... pissed off about the belt."

Robbie reached out again for his shoulders and Jamie pushed him away.

"Robbie, fuck," he said.

"We'll get it back, Champ," Mo said. "When you're better."

Jamie looked up. "Don't call me Champ anymore." He stood and marched down the narrow hall.

The kid was in the ring now. He'd left the heavy bag even though Jamie had told him to keep at it.

Jamie jumped up onto the edge of the ring and slid through the ropes. The ring squeaked under his weight and gave him a little bounce in his step. It was sunny for this time of year and the light came in through the high windows and shone down on them in the ring like a spotlight.

"What are you doing in here, kid? You don't follow instructions, you get hurt."

"Robbie told me..."

"You've got to follow instructions. Show me that double."

The kid fired the double jab and kept his hand up this time.

"Do it again. And again." And on the third time, when the kid was getting into it and working on instinct again, he dropped his hand.

"Kid, fucking listen. Keep that hand up. You understand me?"

"Yes, Coach."

"I'm not your fucking coach. And I'm serious. You're gonna get hurt, and then all of this will go away. Everything."

"Yes, C—Yes."

"Square up on me. Now show me that jab again, at me."

The kid was nervous. Clearly. His breathing was jagged even though he wasn't tired.

He pumped those first jabs out at maybe a quarter speed, didn't even let them land.

"I'm not fucking made of glass, kid. Now do what I said. This is important."

The kid fired the double jab, and Jamie slipped them both, and the kid dropped his right hand, and Jamie brought his open hand up light and tapped the kid on the cheek.

"You drop your right and you leave yourself open to the left hook. Hear me?"

"Yes, Coach."

"Don't say 'Yes, Coach,' just fucking do it, okay? Just fucking do it. You're going to get hurt."

"Y-Yes. Yes, Coach."

"Again."

The kid fired the double jab again, and again he dropped his right on the second shot, and again Jamie slid out of the way and slapped him across the cheek, harder now.

The kid blinked and then blinked again. He nodded at Jamie, and Jamie nodded back, and the kid fired the jab and dropped his hand, and Jamie threw the counter left slap to the face, landing flush against the kid's reddening cheek.

The kid became more and more frustrated—at which of the two of them, Jamie didn't know. He threw faster and faster, growing sloppier and sloppier, and dropping his guard more and more the wilder he got. And each time Jamie slipped every jab and slapped the kid, open palmed across the cheek, leaving a brightening red flash across the pale skin.

The kid was teary eyed.

"Hey, take it easy, guys!" said Mo. He and Robbie were hanging over the ropes, the concern clear across their faces.

"The kid's gonna get himself hurt," Jamie said. "And then what will he have?"

Mo sucked a breath in through his teeth like he had in his office, like it caused him pain somehow to watch him.

And that's when he felt the kiss of leather on his chin and felt his neck snap back—and then almost immediately after, felt the sting of impact on his left palm.

He was still looking at Mo and Robbie, and none of them made a sound—not right away, and not a second later when the kid tried to pull himself up off the canvas and stumbled back to his knees, glassy eyed and staring off into the distance.

Jamie had taken his eye off the kid to look at Mo and Robbie, and the kid had landed on him, and Jamie had fired a left hook on instinct. It was open handed, but it was hard. He hadn't meant to. It just happened.

The kid pawed his fist through the air, trying to reach a rope to pull himself up, but he couldn't judge the distance of it, waved his arms above him in the middle of the ring like he was drowning, and Jamie stood above him, red faced now and frozen, lungs shuddering, while Mo and Robbie ducked in through the ropes in slow motion.

**JAMIE WAS HUNCHED OVER AND** leaned up against the wall by the front door of the gym when Mo came out. Jamie had grabbed a gym hoodie off a chair on the way out—not sure whose—and buried his hands in the pouch, but Mo was in just a T-shirt, and he immediately started clapping and rubbing his hands together, shuffling from foot to foot.

"Sorry, Mo. It was an accident."

"An accident, yeah. I saw."

"It was. I got distracted and he hit me and then I threw on instinct. It's what you always told me."

"I know it is."

"Your nose is a button, you said."

"It gets pressed, you fire back."

"I didn't mean to, Mo. Let me go and tell the kid."

Mo held up a hand. "No. You don't go tell him nothing."

"Well, what am I supposed to do then?"

Mo stepped to him and slapped him on the shoulder. "It's cold out here," he said. He dabbed at his eyes with the back of his hands. "The cold," he said. Then he said, "Take a break. Give it some time."

"Time for what, Mo? I'm still fast. I'm still strong. I'm ready."

"Right, too ready. Take some time."

"And do what? Just go home?"

Mo crossed his arms and rubbed them to bring the heat back. He shrugged, as much as he was able. "Sure, boy. If that's what you want. Just take some time."

"Fuck you, Mo. This is my home."

Mo stepped toward him again, but Jamie backed away from him, his feet shuffling across the pavement.

"Yeah, and my home, too. And Robbie's. And that kid's."

"Did he put you up to this?" he asked.

"Who?" Mo said. "The kid? No."

Jamie watched the traffic crawl by as if everything were normal. He kept watching them go wherever they were going when he felt a hand clasp his shoulder, and he kept watching it when the hand lifted off and when he heard Mo walk back inside and the door close.

In the pouch of the hoodie, he made fists and he swore, and his right hand throbbed uselessly, deep in the bones.

# Chapter 9

AT SOME POINT IN THE night he went downstairs. It was cloudy and the streetlights out front wouldn't have reached that far back into the house, even if they were working. So he made his way down by touch and memory, and found the bottle by feeling blind across the counter and then stood there and drank it in the dark, leaning with his back against the kitchen counter. It had been more than a week since he'd told Sid he'd go with him. He hadn't been able to bear being sober since.

Sid could have got the lights back on by now if he'd wanted, but it made him laugh whenever he came back home, Jamie standing alone in the dark and waiting.

There was no way to know how long he'd been downstairs for sure, but he'd taken quite a few drinks, and his knees and back had started aching from the standing and then stopped aching from the whisky, when the neighbours' motion sensing light flashed on and their cat walked down the top of their fence and stopped in front of Jamie's kitchen window.

"Hey, cat," he said and stepped toward it, loose legged, and knocked on the window. What's-her-name who interviewed him and thought he was an idiot, she had cats. He'd seen the hair on her sleeve. He knocked on the window again. The cat didn't move, though he thought he heard a grunt coming from upstairs in Sid's room. He left the window alone and opened the back door and blew kisses to the cat on the fence, but it just crouched down and looked at him.

The fridge was warm with the power out, but there hadn't been much in there anyway except two half-full bottles of barbecue sauce, some sachets of ketchup, and a petrified onion in the bottom drawer. He pulled a Styrofoam container with a pita in it his brother had gotten him for dinner. He hadn't been hungry for several days. He'd lost a bit of the weight he'd gained. And he got drunk even easier.

The pita was stale and the salad all wilted, but the shaved, grey meat looked the same as it had when his brother had brought it home. He stripped it from the container with his fingers and put it into a little pink, plastic cereal bowl he pulled from under the counter.

"What else do you like?" he said to the cat, which was still just sitting there. The light flicked out and Jamie waved his hands from the doorway to bring it back to life.

There were cans of tuna in the cupboard and Jamie peeled the top off one of them and used his fingers to shovel it from the can into the bowl with the shaved grey meat.

"Fuck," he said, and stuck his finger between his lips, his mouth filling with the copper taste of blood and the briny taste of the tuna water. He dug his finger back into the can and scraped out the rest.

"Cats are meat eaters, right? You're not going to give a shit."

He used his finger to stir it all around and he had another drink and then he went to the back door. The light flicked off. He waved it on. The cat looked over at him and he held the bowl out.

"Hey, I made you food. And fuck that Holly, hey? You'll like this."

He stepped toward the cat, bowl outstretched, and it leapt off the fence, disappearing into the dark of his neighbours' yard. Jamie stood by the fence with the bowl in one hand

and his drink in another until his knee flared up again and he sat down in the doorway.

"I looked up Tamura on Sid's phone, hey cat? He's got a title fight booked now. A fucking title fight. What do you think of that?"

He looked down at the bowl in his hand and had no idea how he would explain it to Sid, so he pinched portions of meat from the bowl and dropped them into his mouth, but he was drunk and it was slick with mayo from the pita or brine from the tuna or blood from his finger, he didn't know, and he dropped a lot—on the ground, on his shirt, everywhere.

It tasted better than he expected, but nothing even close to good, and after a few mouthfuls threatened to turn his stomach he threw the bowl into the neighbours' yard and went back inside, laying out on the sofa and every once in a while pouring himself a mouthful of Worthy's.

When the sun came up, he sat up and made a coffee that he poured a healthy dose of whisky into. He sat on the couch in the living room—dusty from their having knocked the walls down, awkwardly placed for their having done nothing else, in shadow for Sid not having restored power to this half of the house—and drank the coffee, staring at the unframed photo of them and their dad on the bookshelf. And when he was done with that he slid down on the sofa, smearing the drywall dust that still covered every surface in the room, and he drifted off to sleep.

"SHOULD HAVE INVITED ME," SID said, and Jamie shot upright again.

Jamie curled halfway back down. "What?"

"To your party," Sid said. He picked up the Worthy's from the floor and took a pull from the bottle.

"What time is it?" Jamie asked. He squinted out the back window. There was light coming in now, a lot of it, but he still hadn't relearned how to tell the time by it.

"Late afternoon."

"Shit."

"Got several hours before we've got to go. Maybe you could use some of that time to shower."

Jamie relaxed into the arm of the sofa, settling in.

Sid raised his eyebrow at him and smiled and brought another bottle and dropped onto the sofa beside him, a burst of chalk dust surrounding him.

"So we meet the man in the church basement at eleven."

"The church?"

"Nobody looks there for devious shit, no matter how much there is, and not just from us. Don't even get me started on all the church folks. The man bought himself a key. They just sold it to him. Didn't even pretend to care what he was going to do with it."

"The church."

"You got yourself brain damage on the way to your world championship? Yes, the church. But like I said, you won't have to do nothing. Just stand there and be a big shot. Keep telling everyone you're a world champion."

"Yeah," Jamie said. "Got it." Then he got up to go to the bathroom. Sid kept the toilet paper on the top of the cistern. There was a little arm for it attached to the wall, but Sid didn't bother. The cardboard tubes from depleted rolls were a pile in the corner. He pissed and then threw up a mix of whisky and the pathetic mess he'd mixed for himself in the bowl some hours earlier until tears streamed from his eyes.

His legs came down a bit crooked as he walked back out to the sofa and sat with Sid and they stared at each other, the house quiet except for the sound of the draft that moved through it different now the walls were down.

His head bobbed loose on his shoulders like he was dodging punches that no one was doing him the kindness of throwing. Sid looked at him through narrow eyes that

Jamie still hadn't relearned to read. Jamie raised the cup to his lips almost compulsively.

"Why you drinking like this? Not that I'm complaining, but."

"I don't think I could go through with this otherwise."

"Just think of the money," Sid said. "You look shook. You gotta get paid, right? Think of the money. Get your worth. Get paid."

"Yeah, sure."

"Have another drink, then, if that's what it takes," Sid said. He raised the bottle, his hands still sure even though it seemed like so much of it was in him already. He poured it into Jamie's mug. He was good for not spilling. "Say when."

Jamie didn't say when, and Sid didn't flinch, and it was only when the liquor overflowed that Jamie said, "When, alright. When. When, I said. Fuck." He moved his mug out of the way, but Sid waited a moment, the whisky falling out onto Jamie's jeans before Sid righted the bottle.

Jamie stood when he felt the wet fabric against his skin. His legs gave out from under him and he stumbled, legs wobbling like he'd been hit with a knockout blow and just hadn't realized it yet and dropped to all fours.

Sid laughed.

Jamie reached out to steady himself against the wall that was no longer there, pawing his hand against the open air. He crawled to the door, sat up against it, pulled his shoes on.

"Where you going then?"

Jamie finished what he hadn't spilled of his drink and tossed the mug along the carpet toward the sofa. "If I don't get out of here now, I don't think I'm gonna be able to later."

"Nah, don't go. I'll get you there."

"I've got to. I've got to get some air."

Sid stood up. Jamie thought he saw him have to steady himself too, but he didn't trust his perception enough to be sure. "You've got to be there," Sid said.

"I will." Jamie raised himself up with the help of the door handle. He opened it. He took a deep breath.

"No, you *have to*. I vouched for you."

Jamie nodded. He stepped outside and closed the door behind him. It was cool, and he hoped it would wake him up.

Sid yelled to him through the door, "I can't go there on my own now. I need you." His voice sounded weak, like it was coming to him from somewhere else.

The wind felt good in his face. He needed more of it. He walked away from the house, past the garbage bin, over the edge of which slumped the old brown heavy bag, chain hanging down to the ground. He kept walking. One foot in front of the other, though often in slanted or crooked lines, up to the headland, right to the cliff edge behind the hospital. It was sunset by the time he got there, and the hospital was closed.

There's a way fights can end that's called "retirement," when a fighter doesn't have enough left in them to get up from their stool at the start of a new round. He "retires" when he goes back to his corner after a round and just does not come back out of it. It's not a submission or a knockout or a disqualification. It's just an inability to take any more abuse, an understanding that there's no real chance of winning, of getting a result he can live with.

He edged forward, shaky legged and wobble headed, until his toes began to press up against the line of long grass that grew right at the edge of the headland, where it was too dangerous or otherwise impossible to mow.

He knew he didn't have the skills to win anymore and didn't seem to have the stomach to lose. If he couldn't fight anymore, couldn't be a fighter, then maybe he should just... retire.

He tried to peek down and over, to really see the drop that one day, half a lifetime ago, he and Sid had shaken their brother's ashes out over. Dex had been cremated because that's what the government paid for when you couldn't afford it, and they poured him out themselves because their father had gotten too drunk that morning and yelled at them from the living room floor. They'd left without him and later just lied and told him that he'd been there with them, and he'd been too embarrassed to challenge them about it. The cliff had seemed higher then, the ocean bigger.

He held his arms out to steady himself. He closed his eyes. He smelled the salt and listened to the wind howl.

Maybe he'd just close the door on this whole thing, as easy as he'd closed the door to his house earlier. But then he remembered Sid behind that door, hollow and distant, saying—almost whispering—*I need you*. He needed to help Sid. He'd already failed to do that once. And he hadn't helped Dex either, who no matter what Sid said, Jamie knew would have turned into a great person.

He stumbled a few steps back, landed on his ass, spent a few moments sitting dazed, trying to accept that this was really all he was left with, and he really had to do it. He crawled to his feet and shuffled back away from the edge, back toward town.

He stopped at the hospital doors. They were locked. He wondered at first if the doc was still in there somewhere, but the lights were off. The only face looking back at him was his own, his ghostly reflection in the glass. Hair too long. Unshaven. Eyes bloodshot, dark ringed. Cheeks fat and pale.

His plaque glinted at him from the other side of the doors.

The door frame was steel with large, safety glass windows. There was a button at the side that would open them automatically. He pressed it and the door clicked against its locks and stayed shut. He pressed it again and again. He pulled the door, shook it against the lock. He braced a foot against one door, pulled against it. He felt it give, a little, but not enough. He took a step back and drove his foot into the glass. It flexed under the pressure. He lost his balance and stumbled, landing knee first on the concrete. When he got back up, he did it again. The window bowed. He staggered. The third kick he threw sent cracks through the windowpane like a lightning strike and popped the window out the back of the door frame. Jamie was kind of proud of himself; he'd never been much of a kicker.

He stepped then fell through the hole he'd kicked in the door. When he got up, he turned to the plaque. He jostled it and rattled it and it came away from the wall where it had been hung from a single screw. If he'd tripped an alarm anywhere, he couldn't hear it. Maybe it was silent. Maybe they just couldn't afford one.

He chucked the plaque out through the hole he'd made and picked it up on his way out and walked around behind the hospital to the edge of the headland. *With gratitude to middleweight champion James Stuart, our friend*, it said.

He threw it, as hard as he could. He'd never played any ball sports, so he just threw it like he was throwing a spinning back fist. It was kind of a shit throw—wobbly and shorter than he'd have expected—but it was more than enough to carry it over the edge and down into the water crashing beneath.

**HE MIGHT HAVE GONE DOWN** every street in town by the time he got to the church. He staggered, head bowed, watching his feet strike the pavement, until his vision stopped blurring so much when he turned his head, until his feet landed more or less where he'd wanted them to, and his head ached with clarity and his stomach boiled.

He wasn't late, but he had no idea how early he was. He sat on the bench down the street. He'd just wait until Sid arrived. If he went anywhere else, he wouldn't come back, he knew. Not the bar, not home. He'd drink whatever there was to drink and wouldn't get up from the stool or couch when the time came.

He started to drift off a bit, so he scuffed his foot against the concrete to keep himself awake for so long that it seemed like he should have worn a footprint in it like those old church steps that bow in the middle from centuries of use, and his shoe felt weird against the ground now as if he'd stripped the sole uneven. He needed to stop doing that; he didn't have another pair.

When he looked up, two men were standing at the top of the stairs leading down to the church basement, smoking the way people had been when he'd come by almost two weeks earlier, so he could admit he didn't know karate and watch kids fall over. Both men were thin. One was taller than Jamie, the other shorter. He didn't think he recognized either of them. They occasionally seemed to exchange a few brief words, but they spent most of the time smoking in silence, lighting one after the other until a third man approached them. He wore a jean jacket, buttoned all the way up, and a toque. Jamie readied himself to walk over. This must be the start of it.

But the third person, Jamie realized now, was even shorter than the shorter man, way too short to be Sid, and he kept a little distance. He said something to them, and then they engaged a few words with each other, and then the taller man walked over and pulled something from his inside pocket. He handed it over and took some money in exchange.

The third man walked away from the other two, down the street toward Jamie. The denim jacket he wore was old and far too big for him, the unfilled mass of it flapping in the wind like a flag on a flagpole. It wasn't even a man. It was a teenager, a boy. Long strands of hair fanned about his face. From a distance he looked like Dex. The ages weren't right; Dex would be in his mid-late twenties now. Not some teenager. But Jamie always saw him young, even when he imagined what he'd have been like if he'd gotten older. Always youthful, always innocent. No matter what Sid said. And here he was now walking toward him, pale cheeked, bright eyes glistening. And he'd just bought drugs from the two guys who Jamie was probably going to help, to take money from.

Jamie looked down at his feet. He wanted to be there to help Sid the way he hadn't before, but this boy, this other Dex, surely he needed protecting too. He needed someone to stand up for what was right, to give him the room he needed to grow up good.

A gob of spit splashed on the outside of Jamie's shoe. The boy was walking past him.

"Fucking bum," he said. His skin wasn't youthful and rosy-cheeked. It was ghost-white where it wasn't spotted with sores, some older and some open. His eyes were sunk and dark ringed. He sneered.

Jamie expected the spit to slide from his shoe, but it just stuck to the side. It was thick. Maybe Sid had been right about Dex after all, that it all would have gotten beaten out of him too. And instead of digging his heels in like Sid or running away to regroup like Jamie, he'd just have gotten smaller and smaller until he did street drugs and looked half like he'd already died.

He shook his shoe more or less dry. When he looked back, Sid had joined the men outside the church, but he wasn't in conversation with them. He was looking up the street, and down it, into the little park across the way, at Jamie on the bench, trying to see if it was him. He looked at his phone three times in the same minute.

Jamie dragged himself over to them, his stomach lurching and his head aching as if his brain was swelling inside his skull. He was already getting a hangover.

There was a light above the church basement door that shone on the stairs and he could see them all by it. The two guys who had been waiting there were wearing suits and coats. Sid had another jogging suit on, the sleeves pushed up almost to the elbows, his tattoos stark against his pale skin, but still muddy looking. He looked squintier than usual, held his arms a little away from his sides as if they were being pressed out by lats he didn't really have, curled his hands to fists. He was trying to look tough.

And actually, he did kind of look tough, at least compared to these other two. He had a scar on his cheekbone that caught the light coming up from the basement, a slight bruise under the eye on the same side. Jamie didn't know where it had come from.

"See? What'd I say?" Sid said. "I told you. Middleweight champion. Just like I said."

The little guy's suit was a cheap one. Mo had arranged for Jamie to get a new suit custom tailored before they went to Japan—he didn't know what ever happened to it—so he knew the difference. When the little guy took a drag off his cigarette, he had a whole map of lines in his skin that spread out from the corners of his mouth like spider webs, went across his cheeks to the corners of his eyes.

The taller guy was very clean shaven, both face and head. The only hair on him was eyebrows. He was thin, but his skin hung loose, his cheeks bottom-heavy and sagging, pushing past the borders of his narrow jaw. He had a suit on too, a bit too short and too wide for him, like it had been for someone else, like he'd stolen it off a corpse.

"Ah, the man I've heard so much about. Put 'er there," the little guy said, extending his hands. His words were easy, but there was no warmth to them. His voice was flat, businesslike. "You can call me Philip."

Jamie hesitated. He was out of the habit of shaking hands. Sid's eyes widened. Jamie shook, and Philip tried to squeeze him hard and hurt him the way some people do, the way he'd been trying to avoid, but he wasn't strong, and it didn't feel like much.

"Big tough guy," Philip said. "Real strong. Hey, John, come and shake this guy's hand. Come and get a load of how strong he is. Might even be stronger than you."

The taller, bald man, took Jamie's hand, and Jamie had to fight not to wince, not to call out. It felt like the bones in his hand were being shifted around. He didn't look like much, this guy, but that didn't always tell the whole story.

He had tattoos, black dots on the meaty bit between the knuckles of his thumb and first finger, and they were also muddy, the ink having bled out from each of them.

Jamie tried to pull his hand back, and John tried to hold on to it, but even though his grip was stronger, at least on that side, Jamie was stronger in the arm and used that and a carefully timed step backwards to put John off balance.

John straightened up and smiled. "Yeah, big tough guy," he said.

Probably couldn't fight for shit, but he was strong and had a reach advantage on Jamie, which was more of an advantage than most would have.

Sid nodded to him. He seemed to approve, but Jamie wasn't sure his brother even understood the interaction he'd just seen.

John unlocked the door and flipped the switch on the wall and the lights flickered on one by one as they entered, slowly and intermittently bringing ugly light to the room. The thin-legged tables and chairs had been placed back in the middle.

The two men walked to the back of the room where they hunched over in conversation. Sid had Jamie stand with him closer to the door.

"See? All good," he said. His face looked like it had been flattened out over time. He'd seen that before. Break a nose too many times and it stops bouncing back. He clapped Jamie on the arm. "All good."

"I've been here before, a couple weeks ago. I never said. Thought I might help teach martial arts, but it was just karate. There were kids here."

There was a clock on the far wall; he couldn't see the hands, but he could hear it ticking. There was a collection of photos, about five of them, all tight together on one part of the wall, Jesus and Mary and all of them, each in a different frame.

One of the men checked his phone. "They'll be here in about ten minutes, then we'll get it done and you'll get paid."

Sid sucked air through his clenched teeth. He used to do that as a kid when they were fighting their dad. It's how he'd stopped himself from screaming.

It smelled like damp and stale sweat in there. There was a sign hanging from the ceiling in front of the door. It was white with red lettering. It said EXIT.

"There was a kid outside tonight," Jamie said. "Looked like Dex." He heard Mo speaking to him then from a long time ago, when he'd booked his first fight, sitting backs against the brick under the steel blue of the rising sun. *That kid, he doesn't know you, but he needs you,* he'd said.

"Huh." Sid shrugged, but his shoulders stayed hunched up. He folded his arms across his chest.

"We could just go, you know. We don't have to do this."

"Don't," Sid said. "Don't do it. Don't leave. Don't just leave again."

"I'm not saying me, I'm saying us."

"Don't."

"Okay," Jamie said.

Sid let out a slow breath, which carried so much whisky on it Jamie almost felt himself getting drunk again. It mixed with the damp and sweat already in the air. He didn't feel good.

The men in the suits walked over.

"I'm excited," Philip said. "I've got both the brothers now. And one a world champion." He laughed the laugh of a used car salesman. "I've got a world champion under me now. The four amigos. Is that it? Four amigos? Four musketeers? Well, whatever it is, I've got a world champion now, and our colleague is going to shit when he sees."

"Yeah," John said. "Shit." John leaned down over them. He smiled. His teeth were bright and perfect—obviously fakes. Jamie wondered how he'd lost them.

Sid shrank away from the taller man. The red of the exit sign shined back at Jamie from Sid's eyes.

"We're going to go," Jamie said.

"What?" Philip said.

"No," Sid said.

"Yeah, we're going to go. We're going."

"No," Sid said. He stepped in between Jamie and the others. He held his arms up as if trying to break up a fight. "No, he doesn't mean that. No. He's just nervous."

"I'm not nervous."

"Nerves or no," Philip said, "you're not going anywhere. We've got a deal. Isn't that right, John?"

John nodded, stretched his fingers into fists. "That's right."

"He's just nervous," Sid said.

"I'm not nervous," Jamie said. A long time ago when he was still working a door outside a club in the city and he didn't have any more in his life than he did now, he got a pistol pulled on him by a kid he wouldn't let into the club, all the flashing lights of the street glowing in the raindrops on the barrel of the gun. He had been nervous then. "I'm not nervous, and we are going."

Sid reached out to grab his arm. Jamie let him.

"Both of us," Jamie said. "For good."

"We can talk about this later, gentlemen, but we've got business soon," Philip said. He nodded to John, who slowly slithered his snake fingers around the buttons on his coat. It was heavy and black.

"You going to shoot us in the church basement, with houses all around, and your business partners a few minutes away?" He had been confident when he started, but when he finished talking and all he heard was the hum of the overhead lights, the rasp of John sliding his jacket off, the ringing of the jacket buttons against the back of the chair that he draped it over, his confidence vanished. His breath stopped. His heart stopped.

"Well, no, we don't shoot you," Philip said.

John stood in between them and the doorway, unbuttoned his cuffs, began rolling his sleeves up. He had tattoos on his forearms as well. Jamie couldn't make them all out. Everything looked blurry. His heart had started beating again. He could feel it in his throat. It was going so fast it didn't seem like it was ever going to stop.

A hand clapped on his shoulder—lightly, but he felt the impact of it all the way down to the bone. His muscles tensed like when he went to the dentist after getting his teeth knocked out and they rooted around in the pits in his gums looking for fragments. His hands clamped involuntarily into fists and they shook.

But the hand was familiar, had comforting scars on it. It was Sid's. The tension dissipated from his muscles, but the shaking remained. It increased, if anything. Sid had locked eyes with John.

"He's just nervous, and we're not going," Sid said, "so everybody can just calm down. And what do you think you're going to do, John? He's not someone you can sneak up behind when he's pissed. He's a goddamned world champion. Come on now."

"Ah, well," Philip said. "John has actually been suggesting to me, Sidney, that your brother was in fact not presently worth the money he's being paid. He thinks that perhaps the very fact that he's here and not back in the ring means he's not, uh, fit for purpose. Isn't that right, John?"

John smiled. "Not much of a grip you've got there."

"Nah, he's fine," Sid said. "Right as rain. Hard as rock. Whatever."

They, all of them, turned their attention to Jamie. Sid was trying to look cool, but the tightness of his lips gave him away. John wanted to fight; Jamie could always tell. But there were unknowns that were giving him pause. Philip wanted to get this resolved and quickly; he kept flicking his eyes to the doorway.

"I'm not nervous," Jamie said, and he was starting to mean it again. This had become a stare-down. A stare-down was a familiar arena. "But me and my brother are going, we're never coming back, and I don't ever want to see either of you again. And you're welcome to test your theory, but you'll lose. And if you go and get a couple friends and come back, you'll lose then too. And if you get bats or knives and come back again, you'll lose then too. Don't you get it? There might be a hundred and fifty people in the world that can beat me, and you don't know any of them. I'm a world champion. Seems like I forgot that for a minute, but you definitely shouldn't."

He took a step toward the door.

John stayed where he was. He slid his right foot back a few inches, so he could drive off it if he threw a punch. This was no longer a weigh-in before a hypothetical fight. This was not a future opponent. This was someone in front of him just begging to be let off the chain.

Jamie'd been lying about being able to take on a big group of guys with weapons, but the rest of what he'd said was true. Or it would have been, if he could use his hand. But he couldn't fight with it, especially without wraps to support it or gloves to take the sting off. It would shatter the moment he touched someone with it. He had one shot, if that, and then it would be gone forever.

Jamie's right leg slid back as well, by instinct. His fists balled up. His right was shaking and weak. It held a fist shape, roughly, but no more than that. He couldn't even have signed his name.

"Go then, before our friends arrive," Philip said. "I'd rather they see only us two than see you departing."

Jamie started walking immediately, head down—John nearly tripped getting out of the way. Sid walked anchored to him, still gripping his shoulder, the way Dex used to, as he walked out the door into the night, up the stairs, and down the dark street without looking up.

"How did you know they weren't going to do something?" Sid asked once they were a ways down the road.

"I didn't. Just wouldn't have been worse than doing that the rest of my life. Dead either way."

A car pulled up to the church and the headlights sent long, thin shadows out ahead of them then plunged them into darkness.

**IN THE MORNING SID WAS** already up. Or, still up. He was leaning over the kitchen counter, watching the rain streak down the window. The sky was heavy with cloud and it was still dark despite being past dawn. Jamie flicked the light switch, but nothing got any brighter.

Sid was smoking a cigarette and ashing into the sink. There was a large, full paper bag on the counter beside him. When Jamie reached the bottom of the doorway, wearing only his underwear, Sid looked over at him, his eyes sunk and red rimmed. There was a three-quarters empty bottle of Worthy's in the sink too, his hand loose on the neck.

"Already?" Jamie asked, though he felt the pull of it himself.

"What's that matter to a guy with no job?"

"You didn't have a job before."

"Not a great one to you, I'm sure. But I got paid."

"You got beat up."

"Sometimes, maybe, but so what? Everyone gets beat. But other times I'd go to a bar and see how people looked at me.

Maybe we can't all be world champions, but I got respect, and I got money. And now I got neither." He took a long drink from the bottle, strangled a cough as he swallowed. He took another. And another.

Jamie reached out to take the bottle from him, but Sid shrugged away, hunched his shoulder up and looked at him side-eyed while he took desperate mouthfuls of the last of the whisky. When he was finished, he threw the plastic bottle on the floor behind him and it clattered hollow and then rolled toward the back door.

He reached into the paper bag and pulled another bottle.

"Went out first thing," he said. "Since I didn't get paid last night and don't look to get paid again, I got what I could get before I couldn't get anything anymore. Two more bottles. Two *last* bottles, maybe, if they decide to visit us again."

"I think they would have last night if they were going to at all."

"Oh, 'cause you're some kind of fucking expert on everything out here."

Sid spit, struggled to take the cap off the new bottle. His grip was loose, and his hands spun impotently around the cap, slipped off and hit the sink, came up with ash painted across the knuckles. Eventually he spun it free and threw it out the window.

"Not going to need that again," he said.

Jamie grabbed the bottle from Sid's hands. Sid tried to spin it away from him, but Jamie had his hand on it almost as quickly as he'd moved. And Sid tried to hold onto it, but Jamie pulled it from his hands as easily as if he'd been a child.

"Sure, take everything," Sid said. He exhaled. A little fleck of spit clung to his bottom lip. He didn't seem to notice. His breaths were shallow, and he looked half-dead in the grey light of the window. His eyelids moved at half speed when he blinked.

Jamie took a deep breath and let it out, and then again, and then raised the bottle to his lips, swallowing it as fast as he could, one mouthful after another, rusty nails tumbling down his throat. He fixed his eyes on Sid's and held them there. He started to cough, really cough, but he kept the bottle where it was and sent it all spilling down his bare chest. His whisky-wet skin was immediately cold, and the spit and liquor soon soaked into the waistband of his underwear. When the bottle was more than half gone and his stomach full and his throat seemed to close up and just not allow any more down it, he lowered his head and hunched over and took a series of long, heaving breaths, before he tried to drink more. When that wouldn't work, he just poured the rest over his head like it was water after a hard session in the gym, and it spattered on the tiles under his bare feet like he was in the showers.

When the bottle was empty, he threw it on the floor with the other and it made the same empty noise as the first. When he looked up at Sid his eyes stung with it and he blinked constantly.

"Get the other one," he said.

Sid just stood there, watching him.

"Fine," Jamie said. Sid reached for the bottle, but it was the same as before. He'd grabbed it through the bag before Sid moved and his brother could not stop him. He took the cap off and threw it out the window. He grabbed his brother high on his arm with his left hand and the bottle with his right. There was still another thin line of purple-flecked bruise that ran from the inside knuckle to the wrist. He wondered if they'd ever go away now.

"Open," he said. His brother stared at him, defiant. He clenched his jaw.

Jamie raised the bottle to his brother's lips and it spilled out over him. He tried to squirm away, but he wouldn't have been able to break Jamie's grip or move his weight around even if he'd been sober. Soon he opened his mouth and was drinking, sucking from the bottle with the same instinctual desperation as a baby from his mother's teat. Needing it, and totally comfortable with that need. A good measure had been lost to his protest before he'd started drinking, but he drank a lot. He lasted a lot longer than Jamie had before he too started coughing and choking on it, before he too turned his head away, and Jamie raised that bottle and emptied the rest over the crown of Sid's head.

When that bottle clattered across the floor, they stared at each other, the draft from the window raising bumps on their skins.

"What the fuck was that?" Sid whimpered, his voice quiet. He bent over the sink, held the back of one of his hands over his mouth, rubbed at his eyes with the other.

"Smoking the whole pack," Jamie said. He shifted around in the nearby drawer and pulled out their dad's old lighter. He flicked the steel lid open and closed.

"What the fuck now," Sid said.

"If I ever see another one of those bottles in this house, I will use it as fuel to burn this fucking place down around us."

Sid didn't say anything, but Jamie thought he might have given the smallest of nods. Sid slid down to the floor, his back against the cabinets, tucked his knees up to his chest almost fetal, and put his head down.

"I need money for Mary," he whispered.

"We'll get it," Jamie said. Sid kept looking up at him with bloodshot eyes, but he didn't say anything. Normally Jamie would have walked away and put some space between them to diffuse the awkwardness. And he didn't know what to say any more this time than he ever had, but he didn't walk away.

He slid down onto the floor beside his brother, back against the cabinet, and put his hand on Sid's shoulder. Sid jerked to try and shake him off, once, and then just settled into it and still neither of them said anything, but Jamie just sat and watched his brother's narrow chest expand and contract slower and slower until it seemed like maybe he'd fallen asleep.

A LITTLE WHILE LATER, HE got to the low stone wall that boundaried it that he'd leapt over previously. He climbed clumsily over the top and rolled down. Many of the gravestones still stood askew, a few seemed to have fallen right over.

Their father's tombstone still jutted from the earth like a broken tooth. Jamie leaned on it, caught his breath. He wiped the water from his forehead, which was still mixed with alcohol from his skin and hair and stung his eyes. It never seemed to run out, never seemed to stop, like a cut that wouldn't close. Or a hand that wouldn't heal.

"Soon there'll be no reason for me to ever think of you again," he said.

Jamie stepped back, lined up, kicked out, fell. He lay on his back, the gravestone almost leaning over him—not like it was checking on him, but like it was gloating. He didn't have the legs for it anymore. Not today at least.

He got back to his hands and knees, crawled over to it, braced his shoulder against it, and drove against it like when he was twelve and his father had taken him and his brothers to the beach to wrestle. Jamie slammed himself against a leg, feet scrambling madly through the ground, gouging tracks into it, and eventually finding the briefest purchase and getting some actual leverage and feeling the earth shifting underneath him, the stone righting, the progress. He slipped and fell, cutting his forehead open on the corner of the stone. He picked himself up, and repeated, and repeated, and repeated.

He didn't know how long it took him, but when he was done and the gravestone stood straighter than most, than it had at least, and the whisky and the blood had been washed from his face into the dirt, he climbed back over the wall and up the hill away from the cemetery without looking back, instead fixing his attention on the path in front of him, making sure he didn't lose his footing as he moved forward.

## September

Those grey scrubs looked loose, but sometimes they still held tight against him when he moved. He wasn't used to wearing them yet, but he found himself pulling against them less as time wore on.

He met Ivan at the closet at the end of the day. He'd come over as a refugee from Yugoslavia a long time ago and then somehow ended up all the way up here. They organized their supplies, cleaned up, did inventory.

"Oh, I've got it for you," Ivan said. He reached down into his backpack and pulled out a clear bottle of clear liquor. At the bottom there was a mass of sprigs and leaves and seeds. "My grandfather's recipe. He used many, uh, many, uh... weeds." He wasn't happy with the word he found, but he knew it was good enough.

Jamie took it and they shook lefts.

"Coming to watch the soccer tonight?" Ivan asked. Once, Ivan had played a lot of soccer, and Jamie guessed he'd been working his way up the rankings when he'd blown out his knee. Now he watched it on TV sometimes, played with his kids on weekends.

"Plans tonight."

"Ah yes, your big secret plans. Okay, well, another time."

"Another time, definitely," Jamie said, and they finished up the rest of their work with Ivan telling him all about the soccer that had happened the past week and all about the soccer that was coming up this next week. It was nice to listen. Jamie had never really had time for any other sports. He had a lot to catch up on.

They slapped hands when they were done, and Ivan went out the back door and Jamie went off toward the front, turning down the hall to Doctor Carroll's office.

She stood when he entered. She grasped him by the shoulders.

He went for his blue chair.

"James. Sit." She pointed to the other office chair at her desk. He eased himself into it. He was still getting used to that too. "How is Sidney?"

"Alright, I think. I hope. I don't really know though, I guess. Not talking to me much right now. Drinking beer now. I think that's better. It's slower anyway. He got the lights back on, and he's looking for work, but no takers. Not sure he'll find any to be honest. Town like this won't be quick to forget. So we've talked about putting the house up when it's all done, though I'm not sure who'd buy it. But he's looking. And I'm making his payments to his kid. So, he's looking."

"Well, I'll keep him in mind if I hear anything. Perhaps I can find a job around my house to be done."

"That's nice of you, but I don't think he'd take it."

"Perhaps not. Regardless, I've been looking into avenues that might provide funding for your project, but I have to be honest that it does not look especially promising at the moment. The government seems to have decided not to 'waste' their time or money on any social programs, especially in this part of the country, and the demand far outweighs supply with the private organizations."

"I'm doing it," he said.

"I believe you will, James."

"No, I mean I'm doing it today. I put up flyers last week. Got no money or anything for it, just doing it free. I just can't wait anymore."

"I can understand that. Well, that's great news. Good for you." And then, after a moment, she said, "The police finally called back. Apparently, since nothing of 'value' was taken, the events here were not a priority."

"Oh, yeah?" he said. He noticed then that one of his shoes was coming untied. He wedged the heel of it onto the edge of the chair and set about retying it.

"Since we haven't been able to afford to fix up the cameras out front, there's no footage for them to watch, so all they could do was ask again if we knew anyone who would want to steal the plaque."

"And what did you tell them?"

"Everyone walked past it on their way in, and it would have been an easy thing to think it was valuable."

"Yeah. Easy mistake to make."

"So unless they find the plaque in someone's possession, it's unlikely anything will come of it. I can't see them being so lucky, do you? Do you think so? That someone would be so foolish as to keep that in their possession?"

Jamie shook his head. "Wouldn't think anyone's likely to ever see it again."

"Well, then I suppose that will be the end of that. Do you have time to sit a while, or must you be off right away?"

"I've got time."

She left him there while she went to the staff room and made two cups of the good pod coffee, and she asked him how he was finding the work.

"It's a job," he said, "I'm not really used to just having a job. Like, *just* a job. But I think it can be fine, if it's not all I've got."

"Thus the rush to get your program off the ground."

He nodded, and then she told him about someone that had come in earlier with a torn rotator cuff, and asked him his opinions on the rehab, and corrected him wherever he was a bit off on the biology or the medicine of it.

When the time he had free ticked down, they stood, and she asked if there was anything she could do for him before he left.

"There is one thing. I need a pen and paper. Nice paper. Can you believe there isn't a pen or paper anywhere in the house? But I've got a letter to write. To an old friend."

"Of course, James." She took a fancy metal pen and a nice notebook from somewhere inside her desk and walked them over to him. "Good luck tonight, James."

"Thanks," he said, and held up the pen. His grip still felt weak and his movements slow, but he didn't think he was in danger of dropping it. "And thanks," he said, gesturing to the paper. "And...thanks."

"Good luck," she said. She hugged him. It was quick, but it was a hug, a real one. As quick as she was, he still had time to touch his head to her shoulder just for a moment. "Good luck."

He dressed in his old sneakers and gym shirt and shorts with joggers and a sweater over them, grabbed his backpack, and walked down to the small beach at the bottom of the hill away from town, along the same path that one day many years earlier he'd climbed down with Sid.

The beach was empty. He was ten minutes early, but he hadn't expected emptiness. There were a few houses this side of the headland. A store. Not much else. It didn't get a lot of light. People didn't like to live there.

A dark-windowed car drove by slow. He tensed. Every time a shadow darkened his doorway or followed behind him on the sidewalk he wondered if it was Philip and John coming back to test their theory about him and his hand and show everyone else in this town that he was no world champion anymore, that he was just some fucking bum like everyone always thought he would be, like his dad had been.

From his bag he pulled a banner. It had his picture on it, the NorthStar Fight Club logo, the logos of businesses that used to sponsor him. They used to hang it over the cage at his back when the announcer called out his name. The car rolled its windows down—a teenager laughing with their friends flicked the butt end of a smoke away—and then it turned away down a road and disappeared.

He found a concrete pylon at the edge of the beach and pinned the flag to it with a rock. He stood with it flapping lightly behind him, looking at the roads, the path, even the water—any way that someone could approach the beach.

While he waited, he kicked his shoes off and his socks and pulled his sweater and shirt off and his sweats until he was down to just his underwear. And he put on his old competition shorts which were dotted with patches of about a dozen companies that officially no longer wanted anything to do with him. He walked into the water—where a long time ago Sid had swum out and Jamie hadn't known if he was coming back—and he waded out against the rising tide as the cold pressed in on him until he stood with the water up to his chest, searching ahead of him for any glint of gold from the plaque. But he saw nothing but an endless sea of dark, growing waves coming in, and he turned his back on it like it was the past, and listened to it roaring and charging behind him, and tried not to break under the weight of it.

Eventually another car stopped in front of the beach and Jamie was wading out of the water and waving before it had even come to a complete stop. A woman got out and lit a smoke and led her two kids from the car over to Jamie. She had curly hair, kind of like Erin. But her curls were bigger, and they looked like she'd put them there herself with a machine or however. She had a puffy black coat on.

"We got the right time?" she asked. "I can't afford to be driving back and forth all night."

"Yeah. Time's right. I'm Jamie."

"There's no one here, Jamie."

"Everyone's here that needs to be," he said.

She looked at the banner and shook his hand and introduced her boys and went back and sat against the hood of her little teal hatchback and smoked and read a book, looking up from the pages occasionally to make sure everything was alright, and smiling when it was.

The boys were brothers. Eleven and twelve. Their hair was slick and shiny. They were all elbows and knees and ribs. He forgot their names as soon as he heard them.

Jamie walked them out onto the beach and with his toe he cut a circle in the sand around them.

"It's cold," the younger of the two said. He was right. If this was a success, Jamie'd have to find an interior space for this. Maybe the church basement.

"Then we'd better get to work," Jamie said. "We're done here when one of you gets me down or gets me out of this circle. Or after an hour."

When the first kid, the older one, planted his shoulder against Jamie's ribs, he froze. He heard his father's voice then, soaking into his brain. "Get your ass down, you little shit." And then he heard Mo's. "What's the matter, boy, coming in high like that?" Neither of those felt right in his throat.

He slid an arm in between him and the boy and peeled him off to the side. The kid stood up and faced him and waited. He was frustrated at being brushed off so easy. He showed it in his scowl, in the way the skin folded at the bridge of his nose. He looked up at Jamie.

The waves crashed in on the shore and they got real loud. The kids' mother looked up from her book, made a move toward standing. Jamie swallowed. The younger of the two tapped the older on the arm.

Jamie looked up the hill where he'd come from, to the hospital. He saw a couple people leaving the building, but they were too far away. He couldn't see them clearly. Someone stood watching him a moment that could have been the doctor, but he couldn't make them out for sure. They stood there and then turned and disappeared out of view. A bit of longer grass waved from the end of the headland. Through the grass he thought he saw another figure, a boy, blond haired and pale. He held up his hand, maybe. Jamie held up his hand to him. And then through a flicker of the grass he was gone. Everyone up there was gone—the building shut, the lights off, the grounds deserted.

In front of him the kids had each taken a step away.

Jamie went down on a knee and they took another.

"You're coming at this problem all wrong," he said. "You're throwing yourself at me like we're the same size, but I've got all the weight in the world compared to you. You got to attack one thing at a time. Come back in but wrap up my leg. Just my leg. And get low. Because you can get down on purpose or I can put you down, but either way you got to get used to fighting your way up from the dirt."

The kids looked at each other again. The older one shot forward, wrapping both his thin arms around Jamie's leg, elbows sticking out, the ridges of his spine rising from under the skin where his neck met his back.

"Good. Now turn, change your angle. If what you're doing's not working, try something else. Swing around to the side of me there. Change approaches. Don't let go. Good. Good. Feel the difference? Good."

They worked, their blood pumping faster until the sweat steamed off them. Jamie told them what he could when they worked against him, and more when he worked them against each other. At the end of the hour, the boys separated from each other and bent over heaving with their hands on their knees. One of the boys tried to spit, and the spit, thick, caught on his lip and stuck to his chin. The other boy laughed. Both of them did. They look backed to Jamie, still giggling.

Jamie stood in front of them, hands on his hips. He smiled, then he looked back up the empty headland again. He didn't know what to do now, how to make an end to this.

# Acknowledgements

Thank you to the team at TouchWood—publisher Tori Elliott, cover designer David Drummond, interior designer Sara Loos, proofreader Senica Maltese, publicist Curtis Samuel, and especially my editor Kate Kennedy, who had more enthusiasm for this project than even I did.

Thank you to those who helped me with the writing of it: Lucy Christopher, who provided me with early feedback and encouragement; Chelsey Flood and Bee Stewart for help refining my later drafts and catching my many stupid mistakes; Paul Russell, who provided me with feedback, several trips to the pub, and the title; Eleanor Walsh, who spent years helping me understand this, puzzling through all my thoughts and problems, while reading about thirty drafts along the way; and especially Rob Magnuson Smith, with me on this from the beginning, who helped me to see that this was about family rather than sport or crime and refused to let me overshoot the ending.

This novel started as a part of my PhD thesis, and for that I'd also like to thank Andy Brown, the examiners of my upgrade and viva, and my colleagues in the Peter Lanyon Building who had their offices open to me.

Thank you to Tristan Connelly—who had the best UFC debut of 2019—for his friendship and stories about Japan.

Thank you to David Zizic for talking fights and injuries with me.

To Kit, Ed, and the rest of the Walshes; Tash Underwood and Andy Wright; Nicky, Jon, and Daisy Ison and the Widcombe Deli crew; and Jo Parson, Rupert Pitt, Jo Woodgate, Nat Bain, Emily Malloy, and everyone else at the White Hart in Widcombe: thank you all for giving me places to call home during the writing of this.

Thank you to all the many members of the Sport Literature Association for welcoming me in, becoming my friends, and giving me opportunities to develop artistically and professionally. Extra special thanks to Angie Abdou, who got me started down this path almost twenty years ago and who has offered me support and guidance many, many times along the way.

Thank you to Paul Springer, Ruth Heholt, Marshall Moore, Craig Barr-Green, Wyl Menmuir, Jo Parsons, David Devanny, Jennifer Young, and everyone else from Falmouth University who have been incredible colleagues and even better friends. And to my students, for being great.

Finally, and most importantly, to my brother Andrew and my mother Moira for their intellectual, financial, and emotional support. I really could not have done this without you.

Originally from British Columbia, **Adrian Markle** teaches creative writing at Falmouth University in Cornwall, UK, where he lives with his partner, the writer Eleanor Walsh. Adrian has published numerous short stories and has recently returned to practicing martial arts. *Bruise* is his first novel.